"Have yo...
that you...

Chase's st...
contrast t... ...esire-laden look he
had worn before. "Good God!" he
exploded. "Do you mean to tell me
you went away with me, were willing
to let me take your virginity, purely to
save a marriage that—"

"I had no intention whatsoever of
sleeping with you," Ashlie yelled,
while she struggled into her dress.
"I know you thought I would, but I
wouldn't have."

"You've just *proved* that, haven't you!
Not two minutes ago, you were mine
for the taking," he snarled. "There
wasn't an iota of resistance."

"Well, there is now!" Ashlie shrieked.

To be reminded of how utterly
without resistance he had made her
was more than she could take. Falling
in love with him had never been part
of her plan....

Books by Jessica Steele

These books may be available at your local bookseller.

Don't miss any of our special offers. Write to us at the
following address for information on our newest releases.

Harlequin Reader Service
P.O. Box 52040, Phoenix, AZ 85072-2040
Canadian address: P.O. Box 2800, Postal Station A,
5170 Yonge St., Willowdale, Ont. M2N 6J3

JESSICA STEELE

a promise to dishonour

Harlequin Books

TORONTO • NEW YORK • LONDON
AMSTERDAM • PARIS • SYDNEY • HAMBURG
STOCKHOLM • ATHENS • TOKYO • MILAN

Harlequin Presents first edition November 1985
ISBN 0-373-10836-2

Original hardcover edition published in 1985
by Mills & Boon Limited

CHAPTER ONE

Ashlie could not deny a niggle of worry when a glance at the sitting-room clock showed it was half past nine. Lynette was late again.

Lynette was her brother Norris's wife, and she had asked her to move in with her seven months ago after Norris had left London to go to work in Brazil. Lynette was lonely, she had said, and Ashlie had her own reasons for making that decision to leave her parents' home in Lincolnshire and move in and keep her company while her sister-in-law waited for Norris to fulfil his two-year contract.

Lynette, at twenty-eight, was a dedicated business woman, and with a few hard edges until one got to know her. But up until a month ago, given that they were totally different types, things had been working out quite well.

But this past month, somehow, although Ashlie could not quite put her finger on why or how, Lynette had changed. Oh, she knew that her sister-in-law had been promoted to the management team at Marriner Security Systems; an off shoot of the mammoth Marriner Industries; and that she was keen to make her mark in her new position. And she knew the transfer to new and larger premises meant that plans, designs, and all other confidential matter had to be moved in top secret, involving only a handful of executive staff so Lynette had to work extraordinarily long hours; but, there was just something different about her just lately.

Ashlie went to remove the casserole from the oven deciding that Lynette would have eaten by the time she came home. The thought struck her as she returned to the sitting room that, where at one time her brother's name was seldom off Lynette's lips, it had been some time now since she had mentioned Norris. Though, since the only time she seemed to see Lynette these days was over the breakfast table, she mused there wasn't much chance for them to discuss anything. She put from her mind the disloyal thought that maybe Lynette thought more of her job than of her husband.

But the disloyal thought that Lynette was more career minded than marriage minded, returned, and would not so easily be dismissed. She had refused to go with Norris to Brazil, hadn't she? But only because, prompted Ashlie's innate fairness, Lynette felt she would be like a fish out of water living anywhere but in a city. Norris knew Lynette better than anyone, even though theirs had been a whirlwind courtship. He was aware his mineralogist work could take him to the back of beyond, and so had decided, when due to leave for Brazil after only six weeks of marriage, that it was better all round, that Lynette should stay in London. Norris was as dedicated to his career as his wife was to hers.

Ashlie could only glean from snippets her sister-in-law had told her from time to time, that Lynette had been not a little put out when, even loving her as he did, Norris had been adamant about completing the contract he had signed only the day before he had met her.

But, Norris had gone, and Lynette with her eye on climbing further up her career ladder had stayed. Within a week of his departure though, Lynette had been on the telephone to Ashlie's home. Both her parents had been out for the evening, and Ashlie had so warmed to Lynette, who had sounded fed up and missing Norris, that she, herself, had opened up and confessed that she too was feeling fed up about her own love life.

'Things not going so smoothly between you and— er—Kevan?' Lynette had managed to dredge up the name of Ashlie's escort at the Register Office.

'We're through,' Ashlie had confessed, the words painful, but accurately summing up the state of her brief romance with Kevan Salter whom she had gone to work with some months before.

'You're not seeing him any longer?'

'He's still my boss,' said Ashlie, 'so I have to see him every day. But, that's as far as I want it to go.'

'Came the old soldier, did he?' queried Lynette. And before Ashlie could decide if she wanted to confide in anyone her shock when, thinking Kevan had proposed marriage, she had discovered he had meant nothing more than that she should be his mistress, Lynette was going on to shake her by saying, 'You don't need his type Ashlie. He had the nerve to tell me—on my wedding day!—that if I felt lonely while Norris was away, that he frequently came up to London.'

'He didn't!' Ashlie had gasped in shock, even though she had seen soon after she had told him she wasn't interested in an affair, that he was the type that no woman was safe from.

'Didn't you know he was a womaniser?' Lynette asked. She was obviously more worldly-wise than Ashlie who, apart from a holiday in Italy, had never been very far from her home town. 'I spotted he was a first class lecher from the moment you introduced us.'

'I know now,' said Ashlie flatly. She understood now the evidence of various women who phoned, or called in at the office, who all received the same treatment that had them thinking, as she had, that they were the only woman in the world, instead of just one of a great number.

'What you want,' said Lynette hearing Ashlie's dull tone, 'is a change of scene.' Then, suddenly, 'I say, why not pack your job in and come to London?' she suggested. But her bright tone faded, as she added, 'To tell you the truth, where once I was more than happy living on my own, it's not the same any more. I could do with your company.' Lynette knew that there was little that Ashlie would not do for her adored thirty-four-year-old brother and she was persuasive. 'Norris would be tickled pink to know you were living here while he's away.'

It had been an agonising decision for Ashlie to make. She would dearly like her absent brother to be 'tickled pink', but, even knowing that Kevan Salter would never be true to any one female, Ashlie had a hard time in making up her mind to cut him completely out of her life.

She wasn't even certain when that decision had been made that she did not want him to talk her out of resigning. But she had gone into his office a few days later and told him that she wanted to leave.

'But why, darling!' he had exclaimed, his face taking on such a horrified expression that she had thought for one wild moment that he must truly love her after all. Then the telephone on his desk had shrilled, and almost in the same breath, she had heard—his horrified look changing to match his suddenly smooth seductive tones—the, 'Why—hello, my sweet,' which he had breathed down the mouthpiece. In the grip of nausea, she had waited only until he had finished making arrangements to go round to his new lady-love's flat that night.

'I want to leave because I'm going to London to live.'

That had been seven months ago. It still hurt Ashlie a little to realise that she had been such a gullible fool to think she, with her short wavy chestnut hair and green eyes, would be the one to change Kevan Salter from the rake he would always be. But at least she could now look back with understanding and blush at the dim little idiot she had been. Though, she supposed as her eyes again slid to the clock, that having gone through the experience, she could be certain of one thing. Much wiser now than she had been, she would be giving the rakes of this world a very wide berth in future.

Not that Ashlie had met any rakes since she had come to London though she knew that that type of man was not restricted to the provinces, she only had to look as far as Lynette's ultimate boss to see that. Chase Marriner, was well named in her opinion. At thirty-seven, he had a reputation that preceded him and made Kevan Salter's infamy pale in comparison.

It was eleven-thirty when Ashlie next looked at the clock, only for her niggle of worry to act up again. Surely Lynette couldn't be working this late? It had been midnight when she had come home last night. But if her sister-in-law had to eat, which meant breaking off and going out with the rest of the team somewhere for a bite, surely, the others had homes to go to!

Anxiety in Ashlie was suddenly to have a heyday when she recalled how Lynette had commented at breakfast how Chase Marriner sometimes dropped in to see how things were going and even to give a hand occasionally. The thought touching nerves, and refusing to leave was that, was he, like Kevan Salter, not averse to attempting to have a fling with one of his staff?

She wished that the thought had never come. But try as she would to oust it, it would not go away. Lynette had told her that only the most beautiful of women were seen out with Chase Marriner, and Lynette herself, with her dark hair and dark eyes, certainly fell into that category.

She told herself she was getting het up over nothing. Lynette had pegged Kevan Salter straight away for the type he was, surely she had more sense than to be taken in if Chase Marriner went after her. Still, Ashlie could find no ease from anxiety. It was no use telling herself either that Lynette was in love with Norris, and that therefore she would be immune to any man's persuasion but his—for Norris was not there.

Ten minutes later, relief surging in to hear her sister-in-law's key in the lock, Ashlie was suddenly ashamed of her suspicions.

'Still up?' Lynette asked, a sparkle in her eyes made it obvious that, tired though she might be after her long day, she had enjoyed her work.

'I thought you might want a snack or something,' Ashlie replied.

'I couldn't eat another thing,' said Lynette with a smile, and added, to have Ashlie's fears rushing in anew, 'Chase Marriner popped in while we were all beavering away. But when my senior told him how hard I'd worked getting stuck into a new and one of the biggest assignments to date, he insisted on a break, and we went and had dinner.'

Ashlie's anxiety peaking, the quick words, 'Just you

and Chase Marriner!' were out before she could stop them.

That Lynette looked startled Ashlie hoped was because she was unused to anyone questioning anything she did. But when, not answering her straight away, a thoughtful look crossed her sister-in-law's face—for all the world as if she was wondering just how much to tell her—Ashlie began to feel all knotted up inside on her brother's behalf. And she became more knotted up than ever when Lynette gave her the answer she did not want.

'Chase is a wonderful dinner companion.'

The next few days were days in which Ashlie's fears were to grow. For since the night when Lynette had as good as admitted that she and Chase Marriner had shared a cosy twosome dinner, she had seen no reason to pretend that she thought him less than a wonderful person. And, even if it was still mainly at breakfast time that Ashlie saw her, it seemed that where once Norris's name had never been off Lynette's lips, Lynette could not utter a sentence now in which Chase Marriner's name did not crop up.

By Thursday evening of the following week, Ashlie had recognised what all the signs were telling her—that Lynette was infatuated with Chase Marriner. But at eleven that night, with Lynette still 'at work' Ashlie went to bed with still no idea of how to tackle the problem, though with an awareness that, for her dear brother's sake, tackle it, she must.

That Lynette would resent her interference, went without saying, for she had lived alone prior to her marriage, and had been completely independent for years before then. That being the case, even if she had been so very sweet to her when she had first moved in that Ashlie had felt some sort of sisterly bond growing between them, Lynette was not going to care very much for her poking her nose into the way she ran her life. The last thing Ashlie wanted was a row, but how could she let Norris down by not so much as saying a word?

Ashlie lay in her bed and wished that Norris was home, dismissing as unthinkable the notion to write to him of her suspicions. What would she be hinting at if she did write any warning letter anyway? Even to herself, Ashlie could not face the idea that her sister-in-law might be on her way to an extra-marital affair.

Her unhappy wonderings in that direction were terminated by the sound of Lynette coming home. But she fell asleep to have nightmarish dreams of Norris angry with her as he sweated it out in upland Brazil, that he was the last to know.

Unrefreshed from her tormented sleep, Ashlie was in the kitchen drinking a cup of tea when Lynette, dressed and ready to get her teeth into another day at the office, joined her the next morning.

'Shall I make you coffee?' Ashlie volunteered. She had time—she was able to leave the flat later than Lynette since she did not have so far to go to work.

'I've just time for a cup,' Lynette thanked her while propping her briefcase up on a chair and checking through its contents.

'You must be exhausted,' Ashlie opined when she had placed a cup of black coffee on the table. 'I know because of the secrecy of your work that the transfer to other offices had to be relatively hush-hush, but,' she paused, 'is it going on for much longer?'

'Not for much longer,' replied Lynette, elegantly taking a sip of her coffee.

'You'll be glad it's the weekend, I expect,' she suggested. Lynette smiled and took another sip of her coffee. Then suddenly, her smile had fallen away.

'Have you written to Norris recently?' she asked abruptly.

'I'm always writing to him,' said Ashlie honestly. But she was aware that where once her letters had been full of what she and Lynette were doing that, unable to lie to him, and afraid to mention too much about Lynette lest she inadvertently revealed something of her anxieties, her last few letters had been filled with any other subject matter.

But, she held down on the impulse to ask if Lynette had written to Norris herself recently, for spending so much time at work, Ashlie didn't see how Lynette could have found the time.

'You haven't told Norris anything about—Chase and me, have you?' Lynette suddenly said.

Ashlie was altogether thrown. Startled, her mouth suddenly dry at the implication behind the question, Ashlie stared appalled. But with Lynette bringing it out into the open like that, she just had to ask then, and risk her being offended that she was prying into her affairs.

'Is there—anything—*to* tell him?'

Lynette turned from her and took up her briefcase. 'Oh, be your age, Ashlie,' she snapped, and left Ashlie staring after her as she went out. The slam of the door was enough to tell her that she had been right to think that her sister-in-law would resent any suggestion of criticism.

Ashlie tried hard that Friday to be the twenty-two years that Lynette had snapped that she should be. But, while coping with dictation, and typing it back, she was to grow a degree resentful herself.

True, she had led a fairly sheltered life, even if she had had her eyes opened to the less innocent side of life in the shape of Kevan Salter urging her to the bedroom door without a sign of a wedding ring. Thank God she had not gone through *that*. But whether it was old-fashioned or whether it wasn't, to her, one's wedding vows must stay inviolate.

She was not so unbending, however, that she couldn't see that when some marriages turned out to be more of a nightmare than the dream that they had promised to be, there wasn't then a sound case for divorce. Nevertheless when she remembered how Lynette and Norris had been on their wedding day, remembered how much in love they had seemed, it angered Ashlie that Lynette should turn on her, and look to be ready to forget that love in her infatuation with that wretched Chase Marriner.

Ashlie calmed down when during the afternoon she got around to thinking that Lynette must still be in love with Norris, or why would it worry her what she had written to him?

Starting to feel better, she had even begun to think she had got it all wrong, and that even if Chase Marriner had taken Lynette out to dinner it could all be perfectly above board. It was no wonder that Chase Marriner's name was forever on Lynette's lips, was it? What with her work being her life while Norris was away, and Chase Marriner forever looking in to see how things were going, what else would Lynette have to talk about? When she remembered Lynette's snappy 'Oh be your age' though, Ashlie was back to worrying again.

Not liking that she seemed to be constantly watching the clock where Lynette was concerned, Ashlie stared moodily into her coffee cup the next morning and wondered if it wouldn't be better all round if she moved out. That way she wouldn't know and worry what time Lynette came home—it had struck two this morning before she had come in!

Never more uncertain about what to do for the best, Ashlie was alerted to the fact that Lynette had at last surfaced, by the sound of her bedroom door opening.

'Thank God for Saturday mornings,' said Lynette affably, as elegant as ever in her smart housecoat when she joined her.

'You did work extra late last night,' Ashlie murmured, not wanting to start the day off on the wrong foot, even if most of the morning had gone by that time.

'Oh I wasn't working the whole time,' Lynette returned, 'I went to a party.'

'A party!' Surprise had Ashlie staring. But, sure that Chase Marriner featured somewhere, it was more slowly that she asked, 'Were there many people there?' Her fears were on the march again when a secretive smile came to Lynette's face, and she answered as she strolled out and towards the bathroom,

'Enough.'

Ashlie rinsed her coffee cup at the sink and wished again that her brother was home. She could not ignore any longer the gut feeling she was having about Lynette and Chase Marriner.

She was trying desperately hard to believe that she might be jumping to conclusions, but when on answering a ring at the door bell, a large bouquet was pushed into her hands by a delivery man, her anxiety was back as severe as before. There was no chance then of thinking she might be making a mountain out of a molehill. For, knowing in advance that the flowers were not for her, when she saw that the attached note was the personal card of Chase Marriner, alarm was to riot through her. It did not quieten when she turned the card over and read his message, that said, 'Thanks for everything'!

Ashlie tried to close her mind to the implication behind that 'Thanks for everything'. But she could not close her mind to the living proof that if Chase Marriner had not already been to bed with Lynette, then, with his reputation—that was his ultimate aim.

A beam of pleasure lit Lynette's face when Ashlie silently handed the bouquet over. But when all she had to say was, 'How lovely,' Ashlie was too choked to voice the question that was begging to be asked. Why is Chase Marriner sending you flowers? She was to have a constant reminder of that 'Thanks for everything' when, unashamedly, Lynette placed the flowers in a couple of vases in the sitting room.

When her sister-in-law went out on Sunday evening, as she had gone out the evening before, Ashlie was so fed up with her thoughts straying again and again to wonder was Lynette out with Chase Marriner, that she looked for some relief in making a phone call to her parents. Though the same incessant nagging worries returned when, her parents obviously not in, her call was unanswered.

But in having thought of her parents, the idea of maybe paying them a visit next weekend suddenly came to her. And, an ever better idea too—perhaps she could get Lynette to go with her.

It was to be Tuesday morning before she saw Lynette for long enough to have any sort of conversation. For, having come home late on Sunday evening, Lynette had been in a rush on Monday morning, and had been late in again that night, so Tuesday was the first chance Ashlie had to put her suggestion.

Though if she *was* having a fling with Chase Marriner, Ashlie considered the small town of Whittledene in Lincolnshire was the last place Lynette

would want to be this coming weekend, so she knew
she had to be careful as she said,

'I thought I might go and see my parents this
weekend. I'd love it if you'd care to come with me.'

The secretive look she had seen before, and was
beginning to hate, was all of a sudden in Lynette's
eyes again. 'You wouldn't like to make it the weekend
after next, would you?' she replied.

Ashlie's heart lifted when she thought Lynette was
suggesting that, although she was working this coming
weekend, she would accompany her the following
weekend. Ashlie smiled:

'That'll be fine by me,' she said, forgetting her fears
and warming to Lynette. But Ashlie was only to
discover that she had got it all wrong when Lynette
next spoke, choosing her words slowly.

'Good—you'll be—less lonely at your parents'—than
if you were here—on your own.'

'Here on my own!' Ashlie repeated shakily, now
aware that whatever Lynette had planned for the
weekend after next, it was not a visit to Whittledene.
'Won't you be here?'

'I'm going away myself that weekend,' said Lynette,
the touch of defiance in the way she said it, causing
hated, but dreadful suspicions to come roaring to the
surface of Ashlie's mind.

But those suspicions, loathesome though she found
them, just refused to lie down. And there was no
chance of her holding back, whether Lynette liked it
or not.

'Are you going on your own?' she asked, hoping
with all her heart that she had got it wrong. But she
was only to be appalled, not to say shattered, when
Lynette replied, still defiant in tone.

'Chase asked me yesterday if I'd like a weekend in

Paris—I told him I would. We're going after work a week next Friday.'

'You're—going to Paris! With *Chase Marriner*! For the weekend!' Horrified, Ashlie stared at the unrepentant Lynette. 'But you—can't,' she gasped.

'Who's going to stop me?' bridled Lynette. Having been her own mistress for so long, she did not care very much to be remonstrated with.

But stunned as Ashlie was, an awareness came to her that in the face of Lynette's defiant attitude, reminding her that she was Norris's wife would only aggravate the situation and would not be of any help in getting her to change her mind. Gulping down further words of protest, she plumped instead for reminding Lynette that it was she herself who had told Ashlie what a philanderer her chosen weekend escort was.

'You must know that Chase Marriner isn't serious about you,' she tried. 'You must know full well that once he's had what he's after, that he'll drop you and go on to the next woman. You told me of his reputation yourself. You said . . .'

'So I did,' Lynette replied shortly. 'I only knew him by reputation before my promotion took me within his orbit. But having got to know him, I've learned that he has that something—special.'

'But what about Norris!' Ashlie was unable to help the exclamation. Lynette had thought Norris had that something special too, otherwise how else could he have swept her off her feet and got her to agree to marry him in such a very short space of time?

'I never expected you to like it, Ashlie,' said Lynette, only marginally less defiant now her husband's name had been brought into the conversation. 'But Norris wouldn't expect me to stay home every night.'

'No, true, he wouldn't,' Ashlie agreed. 'But there's a world of difference between going out for an evening's innocent entertainment, and what you're proposing to do.'

She had expected Lynette to rise at her blunt comment. But when instead, Lynette looked past her and quietly said no more than, 'I can't help myself,' Ashlie was to feel defeated.

'Not even when you know Chase Marriner is probably dating half a dozen other women at the same time,' she made herself return.

'I know he has other women,' Lynette replied, starting to look uptight, 'but it doesn't matter. All that matters,' she added, showing by taking up her briefcase that the discussion, as far as she was concerned, was over, 'is that when I'm with Chase, he can make me feel that for him, other women just don't exist.'

How she got through her work load that day, Ashlie never knew, because her mind was never with her work. Gradually she had to come to terms with the shock of what Lynette had told her that morning, but Ashlie knew unquestionably, that her brother, warm, dependable, though sometimes stubborn, was a man with very firm views on marriage. He was a man who would never forgive his wife committing adultery.

She was still nursing the same worries when, Lynette not being in, she had the flat to herself that night. As far as she knew, Lynette and Chase Marriner may already be lovers, but if not, then surely there must be something that could be done between now and a week next Friday to prevent that from happening. For if Lynette did go away with that diabolical man, then, certainly, when she returned, not only would the affair be on the way to being over but also her marriage. For, whatever else Lynette was, she was as honest as Norris. And, if Lynette had not yet written to Norris about anything that was going on then, whether it be to her detriment or not, Ashlie could not see Lynette hiding from him what she had been up to for long.

Her heart ached with the knowledge that despite the deep love Norris had for his wife, he would be unforgiving when she told him of her brief affair. Ashlie was still unable to see what was to be done to prevent the catastrophe, when the telephone rang. It was her mother.

'I rang you on Sunday, but you were out,' said Ashlie after her greeting.

'We're getting out and about a bit now that your father has retired,' replied Joan Holman. 'Did you ring for anything special?'

'Just for a chat,' said Ashlie, wishing she could confide her worries, but loyalty to Norris held her back—even when the question came.

'How's Lynette?'

'Fine,' she replied. 'She works hard, and . . .'

'Quite a feather in her cap, her promotion,' went on Joan Holman, the pride in her voice for her daughter-in-law's achievement was obvious. But it dipped when, not understanding how any girl could put her career before her son, she went on, 'Such a shame though, that she wouldn't go to Brazil with Norris. It seems a sin when they're so much in love.'

Ashlie murmured some kind of a reply, and afraid that she might let something slip, she quickly got her mother off the subject of Lynette and Norris, by saying that she had thought of coming home for a weekend soon.

'Well don't come this weekend, because your Aunt

Lilian has been poorly, and we're going to spend several days with her from next Saturday,' her mother put her off. 'And after that,' she went on, 'I'm hoping to persuade your father to take me to the coast for a holiday.'

'In February!' Ashlie exclaimed, loving her slightly wacky mother who would see nothing wrong in making snow castles on the beach.

'It'll be March by then—but that's what's so lovely about your father taking early retirement; we don't have to think carefully how to spend his holiday allowance.'

Ashlie said goodbye, her spirits briefly lifted with the thought that life looked like being one long holiday for her parents from now on. But in going over the conversation, and remembering her mother's, 'they're so much in love' she was to know anger that the love which Lynette and Norris had shared, and which should have stood the test of time apart, had little chance of survival when there were such men as that serpent Chase Marriner about.

Her anger against Chase Marriner was on the boil. Ashlie wished again that her much-loved brother was home. For placid though Norris might for the most part be, by no stretch of the imagination would he sit back quietly and let that libertine come in and wreck his marriage.

She dwelt for a delightful moment or two on a picture of Norris going to seek Chase Marriner out, and of her brother laying him flat with a right upper cut to the jaw. But as the picture faded, she had to face up to the fact that Norris wasn't there—nor could she send for him. Besides, even if she did send for him, Lynette could well have been to Paris and back before he received her letter, and in any case, there must be something she could do to prevent Lynette from going away at all. Though the Lord only knew what that could be.

Half-an-hour later Ashlie was still impotently trying to think up some way by which to divert Lynette—who could be equally as stubborn as Norris when she set her mind to anything—from her planned course. But when that thirty minutes had passed she knew with frustration that not one thing had she thought of that was guaranteed to have Lynette changing her stubborn mind.

Angrily she left her chair, sure of the view then that since Norris wasn't there to punch Chase Marriner on the jaw, she would love to go and do it for him.

Abruptly, Ashlie halted. It wasn't such a bad idea at that! Not, she fumed, that she could go and punch him on the jaw, but didn't he have a few home truths coming!

A few more moments ticked by as Ashlie realised that, as Norris's sister, she owed it to him to do *something*. Though Lynette would never forgive her if she went to Chase Marriner's office and created a scene—what was to stop her from going to his home!

In her opinion it was high time that someone told that monster where he got off.

CHAPTER TWO

WHEN, against her nature, Ashlie went prying into her sister-in-law's bedroom, all her guilt was to depart when, on the dressing table, she saw that the personal card that had come with Chase Marriner's flowers, had not been disposed of.

Tears stung her eyes when she turned from making a note of his home in Hertfordshire, and for no reason, his telephone number. Her eyes caught the framed snapshot of Norris on the bedside table. She was more convinced than ever that she was right to interfere. For, despite Lynette planning an unfaithful weekend, to have that snapshot were she would see it on waking each morning, must mean that she still loved Norris.

Still of a mind to go and see Chase Marriner if she could not dissuade Lynette from the Paris trip, over the next few days Ashlie made several attempts to get her to change her plans—but, all to no avail.

Ashlie had come round to see that, since she didn't know which way Chase Marriner would jump, to go for him full throttle from the moment she saw him, might see him digging in his heels and have him more determined than ever to take Lynette away. Whereas, since Lynette could not see that what she was doing was all wrong, if Ashlie went about the confrontation more calmly then, long shot though she thought it, she might be able to appeal to what little sense of decency he had. Maybe then she could get *him* to see that to be Lynette's lover while her husband was thousands of miles away, was hardly cricket.

Ashlie got out of bed on Saturday knowing that her last idea for a course of action was a non-starter. It was precisely because Norris was those thousands of miles away, that Chase Marriner, the swine, was taking advantage.

But as she pattered to the kitchen, she determined that, though banging her head against a brick wall it might be, she had to have another go at Lynette.

Fifteen minutes later, carrying a tray, daintily laid with coffee and toast, all Lynette ever touched in the morning, Ashlie went and lightly tapped on her sister-in-law's bedroom door, then went in.

'I thought I heard you about,' said Lynette, already sitting up, a smile coming to her mouth when she saw the tray Ashlie was carrying.

'You work so hard,' said Ashlie. It was the truth, but it was said more as a lead up to getting to Lynette before she donned her make-up and the sophistication that went with the clothes she wore. 'I thought you might like breakfast in bed.'

'You're sweet,' said Lynette to give Ashlie's conscience a twinge. But before she could get tactfully started on what she was there to say, Lynette was proclaiming, 'Roll on next Friday—I could do with a change. Did I tell you I won't be back until Monday, by the w . . .'

'Lynette, no!' exclaimed Ashlie, her carefully rehearsed words forgotten. 'You can't go. Norris loves you!' she cried, her eyes moved to the snapshot of him still there on the bedside table. But she knew she was fighting a losing battle when a tight look came to Lynette's face.

'I didn't live in a nunnery before I married him,' she snapped.

'But—he won't forgive you—if . . .'

'Do you intend to write and tell him?' Lynette interrupted, and Ashlie could see from her aggressive attitude, that she was just not going to be able to get through to her.

It was thoughts of Norris that prevented Ashlie from going straight out that Saturday and looking round for a flat of her own. For his sake, she just had to stick in there.

But she knew that she had done all she could in the way of getting Lynette to call off her Paris weekend. And on Monday, when Lynette, home early for a change, left the sitting room with the comment, 'I'd better go and sort through my clothes,' Ashlie was aware that she meant to sort through to decide what to take with her at the weekend, and knew that the time had come to get her car out and make it to the other side of London—to Hertfordshire.

'Julie Grant, one of the secretaries at work, is in hospital having her appendix out,' she called to Lynette. 'I'm just off to visit her.'

It was no lie about Julie. But when Ashlie got behind the wheel of her ancient Mini, she had no intention of going anywhere near the hospital.

It was her hope as she sped along, although with men of his kind it wasn't guaranteed, that with Chase Marriner having no date with Lynette that night, that he was not dating anybody else either.

She had not dawdled, but, having taken a wrong turning or two, it was getting on for a couple of hours since she had left the flat before she was pulling up in front of the vast stone fronted building of Clarendon House. With luck, she would find Chase Marriner at home.

She anticipated, when she rang the bell, that anyone but him might answer the door. But when the door was pulled back on its hinges and a tall, fit-looking man stood there, immaculate in a well-cut dinner jacket, she knew instinctively, that he was the man she was there to see.

Objecting strongly to the way his eyes sought to make what they could of her shape in her trousers and car coat, Ashlie strove to keep calm. While waiting for her to state her business, he raised his eyes to give her features another scrutiny.

Stamping on the impulse to start slamming into him on his doorstep, it was politely that she said, 'I wonder if I could see you for a moment or two.' And, as an after thought, 'You are Mr Chase Marriner?'

He nodded, attracting her glance to the well-shaped cut to his light-coloured hair. 'I do have a function to attend,' he remarked, charm there, his tone interested. 'But, I'm sure I can spare you a few moments.'

God help us, she thought, smooth isn't the word. In next to no time she found herself over his threshold and standing in the hall. Though when he made no move to direct her to his drawing room, Ashlie guessed he must be waiting for her to introduce herself.

'I'm Ashlie Holman,' she told him, noting the recognition of her surname in cool grey eyes the moment before he replied. His brain was obviously always in the overdrive position.

'I have a member of staff by the same surname,' he murmured.

Well at least he wasn't pretending, since he must have already gleaned she could well be an in-law of the woman he planned to take away, that he had never heard of Lynette.

'I'm Lynette's sister-in-law,' she said, her watchful green eyes noting that, so practised was he, that when he must have twigged she was there in connection with his intention to take Lynette off for a clandestine weekend, he did not so much as blink. His mouth was even showing the traces of a smile as he suggested that perhaps she would like to follow him.

He led the way to a large, oak panelled, drawing room. His charm was in evidence again when, despite the fact he had 'a function to attend' he invited her to take a seat in one of the several settees in the room. And cool, where she was starting to simmer that he didn't look to be one iota put out—when he *must* know why she was there—he asked if she would care for a drink.

'No thank you,' she replied, still polite. 'Lynette is married to my brother Norris,' she said, to make certain, when there was no doubt in her mind, that he knew exactly why she was there.

'I've not had the pleasure of meeting him,' he replied, in no way ruffled. Obviously not able to see enough of her, 'Would you care to remove your coat?' he suggested.

'I won't delay you longer than necessary,' she refused his suggestion, and not caring a hoot if she had to suffer the extremes in the change of temperature when she went outside. And not intending to delay her departure longer than necessary either, though striving hard not to show her anger, she said, 'You'll have guessed why I'm here, of course.' Pleasantries as far as she was concerned, were over.

She had by then realised that little short of a time-bomb would shake his confident poise, and was not surprised that when confronted he should smile, and look not the slightest disturbed. Charm appeared again. He said good humouredly, 'I'm working on it,' and she knew she was going to be hard put to get her piece said without losing her temper.

With Chase Marriner so affable, so undisturbed, control came to her when it suddenly dawned that since the weekend he had planned was not the kind of thing one broadcast, he could well be of the opinion that Lynette had kept silent about it, particularly to her in-laws. If so, Ashlie thought, it was about time she enlightened him about Lynette's particular brand of honesty.

'I'm here,' she said, begrudgingly giving him the benefit of the doubt, 'about this Paris trip.'

That he did not so much as move an eyelash when it was plain that she knew all about it, but instead allowed his eyes to once more take stock of her features, made Ashlie's anger spurt to the surface. His movement to the drinks table showed her he'd clearly decided that this was going to take longer than he had supposed. That was before he drawled laconically,

'It's this Friday, I believe.'

The swine, she fumed. He knew full well it was this Friday. But it hit home that, be it with some charm, the overbearing confident toad was plainly telling her that since this interview was none of his seeking she could do all the leg work. Any intention she'd had to appeal in a civilised manner to what little sense of decency he had, went flying.

'You know damn well it's *this Friday*,' she flared hotly, no sign of the polite young woman about her. Her green eyes sparked anger as she saw him turn, spirit decanter held aloft, and stare at the sudden aggression emanating from her.

But still his manner was relaxed, even if his eyes were watchful, though there was not a trace of a smile about him she noted when, his tone cool, he remarked evenly,

'You sound very much as though you would prefer Lynette should stay at home.'

Ashlie was appalled by his colossal arrogance. Stunned that he could look at her, the sister of the man he intended to cuckold, without so much as a glimmer of discomfiture and say what he just had, Ashlie was too taken aback for a second to say anything.

'My God!' she exploded. 'Haven't you any conscience *at all*?'

On the way to pouring himself a scotch, he reached for a crystal glass. 'Should I have?' he asked, his voice urbane.

'You don't think,' she stormed, incensed, 'that your taking my brother's wife away for a . . . a dirty little weekend, is anything to have a conscience over?'

The decanter jerked in his hand and splashed some of the scotch on to his other hand. It was the first sign she had seen of any reaction in him. But when, wiping the droplets away, he replaced the decanter and strolled over to where she, in her rage had rocketed from her seat, Ashlie could see no sign whatsoever of his being in any way abashed. Coolly he looked down into her flashing eyes. And just as coolly he commented,

'My, my, you are het up, aren't you?' And before she could let fly the reply that she had every reason to be het up, he asked, a shade thoughtfully, 'Lynette has told you all about it?'

'I suspected something might be going on *before* you sent those flowers thanking her for *everything*,' Ashlie tossed at him waspishly, angry colour staining her cheeks pink.

Still furious, she saw he had remembered sending flowers to Lynette. But she was further peeved when, plainly used to being the one in charge, he took the initiative from her to question when had Lynette confessed about her Paris weekend.

'You challenged your sister-in-law when my flowers arrived?' he queried.

'I—couldn't,' she found herself mumbling. But not liking from his sharp look that he had seen her sensitivity, her aggression reared again, as accusingly she told him, 'Lynette volunteered the information that she's taking off with you to Paris on Friday night.' In the vain hope of making him squirm, she added, 'Behind her husband's back.'

It *was* a vain hope. Not so much as a tiny wriggle was there about Chase Marriner.

'No doubt Lynette holds the view—since you're obviously very fond of your brother—that you wouldn't dream of shattering his illusions while he's sweltering away in Patagonia.'

'Brazil,' Ashlie corrected him crossly. She could see that from her previous reply of 'I couldn't' that Chase Marriner had accurately pegged that truly she couldn't hurt Norris by letting him know what was going on. 'Norris is in Brazil,' she added. But her rage was again let loose when all the tall man in front of her did was to nod; it was obviously entirely immaterial to him where Norris was, so long as he was not around to spoil his plans for his sordid little love affair. 'My stars!' she cried, 'Men like you make me sick.'

'You have so much experience of men like me?' was his silky come back.

'I've enough to know that once you've had your—fun—you'll drop Lynette without a thought, and go on to the next woman to take your eye,' she spat back at him. 'You're the sort who doesn't care who the hell gets hurt, so long as everything in your particular garden is rosy.'

'I'm devastated by your opinion,' he slipped in

mockingly. But Ashlie, having lost her control, had not finished.

'It doesn't matter a scrap to you that my brother's marriage will be in ruins when he hears . . .'

'So you *do* intend to tell him?'

'I wouldn't dream of telling him,' Ashlie said tartly. 'But . . .'

'But you'll make sure he knows?'

'I didn't mean to imply that.' Somehow she was on the defensive and not liking it any more than when he had taken the initiative from her before. 'I meant that Norris is bound to know that Lynette has not kept faith with him. They have that sort of an honest relationship.'

'It sounds like it,' he said shortly. There was no charm about him then, when he added curtly, 'Does Lynette know you're here?'

'Of course she doesn't!' Ashlie exclaimed. 'I told her I was off to visit a sick colleague in hospital.' It annoyed her that in confessing to having lied, it was she who was the one to feel discomforted. But, belligerency came to her aid, and she was then angrily hostile again. 'Not that I needed to lie, Lynette has her head so full of you and what to pack to take to Paris that she probably wouldn't have noticed I'd gone out.'

'Naturally, you've asked her not to come away with me,' he stated, mockery there as he added, 'Even though you know that I'll send her back home when I've—finished with her.'

Her breath taken, 'Why you—callous swine!' she gasped, unable to credit that he could stand there and not baulk from saying it. But, striving to overcome that swine was too good a name for him, 'You've just shown that she means nothing to you,' she said. And swallowing down more ire, the purpose of her visit there inspiring her, 'Please leave her alone, Mr Marriner,' she said trying for calm, 'Lynette would never have gone off the rails if you hadn't tempted her. And I'm sure she'll come to her senses and settle down again—if only you'll call off this Paris trip.'

Her voice had gone to a near imploring tone as she came to an end. But as she observed his eyes fixed to her face, hope soared that from the serious consideration he appeared to be giving her plea, that at last she was getting somewhere.

When the corners of his mouth started to turn upwards, that hope in her faded. And, on the way to thinking once a rake always a rake, she felt humiliated and angry that she had lowered herself to plead, when, he replied, pleasantly, 'But why should I call off the Paris trip? I've been looking forward to . . .'

'I've no doubt you have,' Ashlie shot in, furious that he should humiliate her, furious that the detestable rodent should think only of his own pleasure. 'But there must be half a dozen other women you could take to Paris—it doesn't have to be Lynette.'

Her fury had glanced off him she saw, and his mockery was there again as he drawled, 'Have you been taking a sneaky look at my—availability list?'

'Damn you,' she hissed, wanting to hit him into realising how seriously she wanted him to see the situation. 'Why *can't* you take someone else? Any one of the females you know would suit the bill surely?' Though it suddenly smote her that she was making light of Lynette, which hadn't been her intention. A touch more quietly, she was having to defend, 'I didn't mean to imply that Lynette isn't beautiful. She is, but, she's . . .'

'Spoken for?' he queried. Not waiting for an answer, he added, his eyes surveying her face, 'Come to that,

you're quite something yourself, Miss Holman.'
Almost to himself, his eyes still on her, he murmured,
'It's many a long day since I saw a complexion to
match yours.' And before she could tell him that she
was not in the market for soft soap, all at once his
mouth was turning up in a mocking grin, and he had
rendered her utterly speechless by mockingly suggesting, 'And insolent bitch though I find you—I'll take
you if you like.'

That, as far as Ashlie was concerned, was the end.
She had come to Clarendon House with the sole
intention of trying to get him to change his mind
about taking Lynette to Paris. To have him mockingly
state that he would take her in Lynette's stead, was all
she needed to know that if she stayed there for another
hour trying to appeal to his better self, she would be
wasting her time. He just did not recognise the word
decency.

'Should the day ever dawn that my immunity wore
so thin that I'd be crass enough to forget my low
opinion of philandering types such as you,' she threw
at him with haughty disdain, 'then you still wouldn't
figure on *my* availability list.' She turned swiftly
about, 'I'll see myself out,' she tossed in his general
direction.

Ashlie thought that she had done all she possibly
could to try to preserve Norris's marriage. But the
following morning when complete with a bundle
wanted back from the dry cleaners before Friday
Lynette left the flat, Ashlie was put to wonder—was
there something else she could do?

When lunch time came, having searched fruitlessly
all morning for that 'something else', she was past
caring that when next she saw Lynette, who without

doubt would have been contacted by Chase Marriner that day, she would be all set to have a blazing row with Ashlie for her having dared to interfere.

Somebody had to interfere though, she thought mutinously, her thoughts going on to that tell-tale rat Chase Marriner. He didn't even have the redeeming excuse of being in love with Lynette, she fumed. Unmistakably, he had no feeling for her sister-in-law, or how else could he so much as say, whether mockingly, or otherwise, 'I'll take you if you like'?

Oddly, when she knew he had not meant it seriously, his insulting phrase refused to depart. And for the next ten minutes, Ashlie found herself in the middle of a fantasy where she had taken him up on his offer, only to say a well-brought up 'No, thank you' when, in Paris, he suggested bed.

She came away from her reverie knowing that fantasy was exactly what it was. For, even supposing she could get him to take her to Paris in place of Lynette, at her first intimation that she had a celibate weekend in mind, Chase Marriner would be hot footing it on the trail of Lynette again.

Though having gone into the realms of fantasy in her search for some way to squash Lynette's plans, she was to discover that the notion to take her place would not lie down. What if she could get Chase Marriner to *think* he was taking Ashlie Holman away for the weekend? She pursued it further. All she would have to do then would be to sit and wait for him to collect her. Surely, when Casanova Marriner turned up at the flat and told Lynette, 'It's not you I've called for, but Ashlie,' Lynette with her much looked forward to weekend up the swanee; not to mention the humiliation of it—and Chase Marriner was good at humiliating people—Lynette would soon be over her infatuation for him.

She became quite excited at the idea—until she remembered her own experience of being infatuated with a grade one bluebeard. Countless lies she had swallowed in her brief but painful infatuation with Kevan Salter. And though Lynette was far more wised-up than she had been, when it came to a glib tongue, Chase Marriner could beat Kevan Salter into a cocked hat. In no time flat, she saw, the head of Marriner Industries would soon have Lynette purring again. Hadn't Lynette herself said 'I know he has other women, but it doesn't matter'?

Ashlie let herself into the flat that night having realised that even if she could succeed in getting Chase Marriner to agree to take her to Paris, he was far too wily to call for her.

But, fed up with her world, that phrase that meant absolutely nothing, still refused to let go. 'I'll take you if you like' was still buzzing around in her head as she busied herself preparing the evening meal.

When she found she was thinking on those lines again, and wondering if she could trust him to keep any promise he made if she told him, 'I'll come to Paris with you if you promise to leave my sister-in-law *permanently* alone,' she recalled that, whatever else was said about him; it was also said that he was a man of his word.

The idea of promising to go to Paris with Chase Marriner if he would promise to leave Lynette alone, began to take root. And excitement started to mount in Ashlie again. Even then though, she was aware that he was likely to kick up rough when, his promise given, he discovered that to go to Paris with him was *all* that she had promised.

One look at Lynette when she arrived home, was to send all excitement plummeting. Just a swift glance at

her beautiful, sophisticated sister-in-law, was enough
to show her how far into the realms of fantasy she had
strayed. True, any immature edges had gone from her
since the days of Kevan Salter and six months in
London had done a lot for her, but by no stretch of
the imagination was she likely to get Chase Marriner
to take her to Paris rather than Lynette. Even if he had
said, 'You're quite something yourself.'

Owning surprise that there was no sign of anger in
Lynette at her interference, Ashlie came away from
reminding herself that Chase Marriner's comment had
never been seriously meant anyway, to test the
temperature.

'Had a good day?'

'Not bad,' smiled Lynette. 'Though I've a few
things in my briefcase I have to look through tonight.'

Which meant, thought Ashlie, somewhat cheered,
that Lynette did not have a date with that brute tonight.

They had nearly finished their meal when the urge
came again to find out if, as looked likely, Chase
Marriner had kept quiet about her visit to Clarendon
House last night. It had been fidgeting at her ever
since Lynette had come in.

'Have you seen anything of Chase Marriner today?'
she asked, unable to hold it down any longer.

The change that came over Lynette's expression as
she thought over her day, the dreamy expression she
did not try to hide, gave the answer even before she'd
said a word.

'Oh, yes.' That secretive look coming to her face,
'He has some business to do tonight, otherwise . . .'

She left it there, but Ashlie knew that if Chase had
been free, then the work Lynette had brought home
that evening, would have stayed where it was in her
briefcase.

Automatically Ashlie made the coffee, but her mind was busy, her thoughts again taking off as she wondered, since clearly nothing had been said about her having gone to see him, *had* he been serious with his 'I'll take you if you like'?

'Lynette,' she said, placing a cup of coffee on the table in front of her. 'Don't . . .'

Reading correctly what was coming, Lynette stood up. 'If you're going to start on again about me going to Paris on Friday, then don't,' she said coldly.

'But Lynette . . .'

'I've got work to do.' And picking up her cup and saucer of coffee, Lynette took it with her to her bedroom, and closed the door.

Ashlie did not see her again until breakfast. But having had to accept from her attitude that there would be no getting her to change her mind, Ashlie's love for her brother had her knowing that she just *couldn't* leave it there.

She was left with only one option. Since Lynette would not change her mind about going away with Chase Marriner, then, loathsome though Ashlie found the idea, she was just going to have to pursue that 'I'll take you if you like', and somehow try to get him to change his choice of partners.

It had come to her during her long fretful night that the only reason he had not told Lynette about her visit to his home, was purely because he hadn't seen it as politic when wooing someone else's wife, to remind his paramour, by the mention of a sister-in-law, that she had a husband.

So anxious was Ashlie that, no sooner had Lynette left for her office, she was busily dialling Chase Marriner's home number, silently glad she had thought to note it down.

'I'm afraid Mr Marriner has already left for the day,' a motherly sounding voice informed her. Ashlie guessed it was his housekeeper, for surely such a villain had never had a mother.

Ashlie thanked her, and rang off. Though the moment she reached her place of work, she was again picking up the phone. This time she dialled the head office of Marriner Industries.

But, her call was blocked unless she would give her name which, since the name Holman might ring instant bells if there was any kind of liaison with the offices of Marriner Security Systems, she would not. She got no further than Chase Marriner's secretary.

'Would you ask Mr Marriner to ring his visitor of Monday evening?' Ashlie asked, giving her office number while owning to feeling a bit of an idiot at what she had said.

'Yes, of course,' replied the secretary, with so little hesitation that Ashlie could only assume that she must be used to handling all types of requests from the females of his acquaintance.

'It *is* urgent,' she thought to stress.

'I'll personally see to it that Mr Marriner has your message.' The secretary was unflappably assured.

When the morning dragged by with Ashlie's heart jumping into her mouth every time her phone rang— but only to find it was not him—the confidence that the secretary would not let her down, began to slip. When the minutes slowly ticked by to half past four, with still no call from Chase Marriner, she knew with certainty, that he was just not going to ring.

She told herself, well, she had tried, but clearly Chase Marriner was not interested. It had been a long shot anyway, but she had done all she could.

It was then she discovered that the strong strain of

stubbornness which ran through her brother Norris, had not been inherited by him alone.

A minute later she was ringing through to Marriner Security Systems, and shortly after that, she was speaking with her sister-in-law.

'I thought I'd better ring in case you wondered where I'd got to,' she explained her call. 'I have a date tonight, straight after work,' she lied. But her aversion to telling lies faded from her when, after a moment's pause, Lynette replied, patently seeing no reason not to be open at this late stage,

'That makes two of us.'

'I might be late in,' said Ashlie, trying to keep her tone even, 'very late in.'

'I'll put your electric blanket on if I'm in first,' volunteered Lynette, 'though it's doubtful.'

Ashlie said goodbye, angry, and fed up, and knowing that with waiting until Chase Marriner came home from his date with Lynette and the car journey back to the flat, she would be lucky if she saw her bed at all that night.

In no hurry, she stayed in her office until the cleaning lady arrived. Then conscious, with Friday evening when Lynette flew off with Chase Marriner only forty-eight hours away, that she could not risk waiting another day, she took herself off for a meal, and killed some more time.

It was going on for eleven when she turned into the drive of Clarendon House, and observed that, save for a porch light, the place was in darkness. She drove slowly up past the house and halted her car some way past the front door.

It looked, she thought, as though she might have a long wait. Quite plainly, the housekeeper, had gone to bed. Ashlie would not have minded in the least if she had forgotten to leave the porch light on for the master, if it meant that Chase Marriner might trip and break his neck going up those steps. She realised though that since she didn't want to get the housekeeper out of her warm bed, her waiting would have to be done outside.

It might have been of some help, as she sat through the first half hour of her wait and then the second, if she did not have the near certain feeling that she was on a wild goose chase anyway. But as the cold of the night started to bite she grew even more convinced, when she thought of how Chase Marriner had deliberately ignored her 'urgent' telephone message, that he would further humiliate her by bursting a gut laughing when she told him how she was there to take him up on his offer to take her to Paris in place of Lynette.

Yet, the stubbornness that had taken a grip on her when she had thought that she had done all she could to preserve her brother's future happiness remained. It would not have her giving in to what was growing to be an almost overwhelming impulse to put her car into gear, and to speed away.

Ashlie was still there when, twenty minutes later, car headlights shone up the drive and told her that her waiting was over. But if, as he pulled up, Chase Marriner had spotted her or her car, he made no sign. He left his car and headed to the foot of the steps.

She had not stuck it out for so long only to have him shoot up those steps to close the door on her so in no time she had left her car too, and was scooting after him.

Though when, his back to her, his key already in the door lock, he did not turn around, he made Ashlie aware that he *had* spotted her. And she was to wish she had some nice blunt instrument to hit him over the head with when, his voice filled with sardonic amusement, the words floated down to where she stood behind him, 'We'll have to stop meeting like this, Ashlie Holman.'

He was laughing at her—before she had even started!

CHAPTER THREE

THOUGH uninvited, when Chase Marriner stepped over his threshold, Ashlie crossed over it too. But it was not until after the front door closed, and she had followed him into the drawing room, that he turned and looked at her full square and Ashlie knew she could not go through with it.

Chase Marriner was patiently waiting for her to state why she had been hanging about in the shadows, she knew that. She had thought it was all straight in her head how this conversation was supposed to go, but as she looked at him and saw confidence oozing from every pore, his easy stance, just the very air of his sophistication, defeated her. He was used to women who knew their way around. Women like Lynette, women who worked and played in his sophisticated world.

Everything in her was telling her to get out of there before she made herself a laughing stock. But a spurt of anger that, unspeaking, he was leaving it to her to state her business, came to strengthen her stubborn feet's refusal to move. Ashlie voiced none of the pleasantness which she had intended but spoke, her tone accusing.

'I've been expecting you to telephone me all day.'

'Have you?'

Starting to hate him that it should sound as though she had joined the ranks of a string of females who sat languishing by the phone all day just waiting for him to ring, she found that her stubborn feet were still refusing to march her out through the front door.

'I rang your office asking you to call,' she explained, holding down anger as she sought for tact, 'but you obviously didn't get my message.'

Her tact was unnecessary, making her wonder why she had bothered giving him a loop hole since his reply of, 'I have a very efficient secretary,' told her that even for the sake of politeness, he was not a man to hide behind his secretary's petticoats.

But that he had as good as told her, face to face, that her message had been received and had been deliberately ignored, pushed her anger out from her control. Tact was far from her when bluntly, she snapped: 'If you had anything about you, you'd give up Lynette instead of . . .'

'You know the way out,' he cut her off, distinctly not caring for her choice of words, any more than he cared for a repeat of a conversation they had already been through.

But that mere words should offend him and have him ordering her out when what he was about was so foul, incensed her. And furious then, not with just him, but with herself, that just seeing him had weakly turned her away from her set purpose, Ashlie found a few more words to offend him with.

'Well you're hardly a man are you?' she sneered. 'No real man would seduce a woman behind her husband's back. Only a rat such as you would take advantage of a wife's husband being out of the country . . .'

'Do you leave under your own steam, or do I throw you out?'

His glittering grey eyes told her he was not enamoured of being spoken to the way she had spoken to him. And she could see that if she didn't soon shift herself, then she would soon be feeling his hand on her collar as he frog marched her to the door, and then, threw her down the steps.

When he moved towards her, Ashlie decided not to delay. But it was humiliating to be seen off the premises, even if pride did have her muttering, 'I could do with some fresh air.'

But it was at the front door, regardless that Chase Marriner was breathing down her neck, that Ashlie turned, her stubborn feet digging in and refusing to budge, while the courage she thought she lacked pushed up through her barrier of weakness. And, albeit that sparks were flashing from her eyes and that her tone was barely civil, the words, somehow, were there.

'That offer of yours—the one to take me away in Lynette's stead—what—about it?' she said hotly.

She had fully expected him to be unable to contain his mirth. But as his anger with her left him and the corners of his mouth started to pick up, she thought it was more from the way she had so *unlovingly* flung her agreement to a lovers' weekend that had amused him. She knew that any second now, he was going to fall apart laughing.

But Chase Marriner did not split his sides that she had offered herself in place of her beautiful sister-in-law. And his mouth was back in its firm and—strange that she should think it—attractive shape when, his anger at her insulting him gone, he let his eyes travel over her, just once.

'Dare one hope you're sunnier in bed, than you are out of it?'

Stunned, simply stunned that, if her intelligence was standing up, his sarcastic remark meant that the door was definitely ajar, Ashlie, with her heart pumping painfully at what she was about, saw that if she wanted that door to remain open, then she was going to have to change her sour tune, and fast.

'I'm ...' she began, searching for just the right words, 'I'm not always so ...' She halted, the abhorrence she felt to go anywhere with him getting in the way of the knowledge that she just couldn't afford to let him see the smallest sign of reluctance. 'Normally, I'm more ...'

Again she had come to a stop. But she could have done without his assistance when, his cool look going over her, he chipped in with another comment.

'You appear to be having some difficulty with your vocabulary.' And, a new light coming to his eyes as they flicked to her mouth, 'Perhaps,' he suggested, 'there's another way in which you can express how "normally" you're more ...'

'What do you—mean?' she asked, a shaky feeling inside her that she already knew exactly what he meant. But he did not straight away confirm her suspicions, instead, not moving from where he stood, he asked abruptly,

'How old are you?'

Wondering what tack he was on now, Ashlie saw that now was not the time to delay her answers. 'Twenty-two,' she said promptly, and discovered with his reply that he had not changed tack at all.

'You're an adult, Ashlie Holman. Add that to the fact I've already intimated that if you spend this weekend with me it won't be just a hand-holding weekend, and you'll know exactly what I mean when I say—show me.'

A flare of anger lit within Ashlie that Chase Marriner, not budging an inch, was making her do all the running. He was insisting at any rate, that she go over to him and give him some sort of a kiss to prove her good intent that if he gave up his plans for himself and Lynette, his weekend would not be a waste of his time.

With nothing else for it, Ashlie moved until she was standing close to him. Though it was to take some moments before she had the courage to do what he asked of her. And only by telling herself that if this was what she had to do to preserve her brother's marriage—then so be it—did she move to within body touching distance of the man she hated the very sight of.

But reminding herself that she had kissed before, so, apart from the fact that she loathed the would be recipient, what was so different about kissing one man or another, Ashlie stretched up to kiss him. And, at first, she thought that there was no difference.

But that was before—for the sake of what she was about, her mouth having to touch his more than fleetingly—she suddenly found that Chase Marriner was kissing her back. And then she knew as two strong arms came about her and held her firm, that she was no longer the one in charge, and that Chase, a man who liked to do his own running, had taken over. All at once, she was experiencing what it was like to be kissed by a man who had been around. She had thought that being kissed by Kevan Salter had been quite something. But, Chase Marriner, not satisfied with one kiss, claimed her mouth again. With Kevan she had always managed to retain just sufficient awareness to know where his kisses were leading, but now, suddenly, a warmth was spreading through her that had nothing to do with her being in a centrally heated home after her freezing cold wait outside. And she was having to fight hard to be aware of anything but the sensation being created in her.

Her heart thundering, when Chase took his mouth from hers, Ashlie wanted more. Her lips parted in invitation, a sigh leaving her when, a smile in his eyes, Chase took up that invitation. And by the time he had broken that kiss, his body heat getting through to her, Kevan Salter, Lynette, and even Norris, had faded from her mind.

When Chase pushed her back from him, it was a stunned Ashlie who stared at him, only then conscious when his arms fell to his sides, that somehow, of their own volition, her arms had gone around him and that—she had been clinging on to him!

Her face flamed with colour—had that been *her*? Knowing that, against all odds, in no time flat, Chase Marriner had had her responding so heatedly to him, left Ashlie too winded to be able to find her voice.

But coming rapidly back to earth, she was to remember what all this was about when, after several moments of Chase Marriner giving her a long hard look, she heard his sardonic murmur break:

'It could be a—fun weekend—with you after all.' Still speechless, still trying to get it all together, comprehension started to dawn that she might have won that weekend when, sardonic still, he confirmed it, by adding, 'I'll expect you on Friday.'

Cold sanity rushed in then. But, shocked into sanity as she was, Ashlie felt not the slightest triumph in the victory of having gained what she had been after.

'Y-you want me to come—here?' she managed after a struggle. And with some lingering trace of a previous idea getting through, she asked, 'You wouldn't consider picking me up where I live?'

He was shaking his head before she had finished. And he was again making her do all the running, his overbearing confidence back, not that it had ever left.

'You're the one—in this emancipated world—who did the propositioning.'

He seemed then to think there was little else to be said, for he was going to the front door, his intention to see her out plain. But, having got herself in more of one piece, Ashlie found that even if he had nothing else to say to her before they met again, then *she* had one thing more to say to him before she joined him for that dishonourable weekend.

'I've heard that once you've given your word, you never break it,' she said quickly, the front door already open. But Chase Marriner looking down from his lofty height neither confirmed nor denied her statement, forced her hurriedly on, with no time to look for tact. 'May I have your word that if I go away with you—that is—after I've been away with you, will you promise not to take up with my sister-in-law again.'

Given that what she had asked had come out sounding all blurted and scrambled, Ashlie thought she could not improve on it, and might easily trip herself up if she tried to put it another way.

He knew what she was asking anyway. But she hated him that while making her sweat it out, his eyes should study her face in just a way to make her think she had just blown it. For when it came to his choosing between her and Lynette, she had a dreadful suspicion that her sister-in-law's dark sophisticated beauty, would win hands down.

But, to her immense surprise, suddenly his mouth was picking up at the corners, and there was even a smile in his eyes when, although his tone was regretful, he gave her his answer.

'You drive a hard bargain Ashlie Holman—but—in exchange for you spending a few nights away with me,

I'll guarantee that Lynette will remain my employee, and nothing more.'

Ashlie was grateful the following day that her work was easily within her capabilities, for she had too much on her mind to give her work one hundred per cent concentration.

Last night on her way home she had panicked at what she had committed herself to. And had Lynette not been in bed, she was sure that she would have told her that she had just come from seeing Chase Marriner, and how he had said he would take her to Paris in her place. It had seemed the obvious thing to do—last night.

This morning, after long wakeful hours, she was again certain that, totally infatuated as Lynette must be to put her marriage in jeopardy, she was wide open to be taken in by any line Chase Marriner shot her to explain his actions. And if, by the smallest chance there was any doubt if she should believe him, then wasn't it extremely likely that all she would have achieved would be to spur Lynette on, determined to re-establish herself with him.

Nightmare visions of the whole thing blowing up out of control made Ashlie resign herself to keeping quiet. If she said not a word, neither Lynette nor Norris need ever know about it. Strangely, she trusted Chase Marriner's promise that after the weekend, he would not return to Lynette.

But it had not only been thoughts of whether to confess everything to Lynette that had kept Ashlie awake. And it was no wonder to her that her mind was far from her work.

All that had been needed after she had Chase Marriner's word that he would drop Lynette; and, if she had read his answer correctly, had the assurance that any further promotion Lynette earned would not suffer for it, had been to say good night.

That he had not taken her in his arms again, but had been satisfied with a verbal parting, was something else for which she was extremely grateful. For when she looked back to the nonsense he had made of her when he had held her in his arms and kissed her, she just could *not* get over it! That he should so assault her senses and have her responding to him the way she had both shattered and appalled her.

In an attempt to oust from her mind the way she had been, Ashlie rang her bank to order some French francs. Provided she spent a few nights away with him, Chase had agreed to leave Lynette alone. To Ashlie's way of thinking, the amount of currency she had ordered should be sufficient to pay her air fare home when she and her weekend escort fell out when he discovered that spend a few nights away with him she might, but that his bed was not going to be her bed.

She was though, indelibly aware of the mess he made of her rational thinking when he had her in his arms—she hadn't been thinking at all last night. She knew that above all else, while trying to keep him sweet while they were still on English soil and it easy for him to reach Lynette, that she must not let him kiss her again.

But if Ashlie had any last minute thoughts on the wisdom of what she was doing, those thoughts were to go scampering away when, after they had eaten that night, Lynette stood up and told her she was going to her room to pack.

'You're going to pack!' she exclaimed, and received a look from Lynette that clearly told her not to again try to get her to change her mind.

'There's no need to sound so surprised,' said Lynette a shade sharply, entirely unaware that Ashlie's surprise stemmed only from the fact that Chase Marriner, clearly not intending to lose out on taking one of them off for the weekend, had not yet told Lynette that she would have no need of her passport. 'You've known for over a week,' she went on, 'that I'll be taking a Paris flight straight from my office tomorrow night, so don't . . .'

'It wasn't that,' said Ashlie quickly, despite what her sister-in-law was about, feeling an unexpected sympathy for her that Chase Marriner was going to so callously let her down. 'It was just that—I'd forgotten that I'll be going away straight from work tomorrow myself, and that I ought to do some packing too.'

She had made it to her bedroom door before Lynette, looking apologetic for having been ready to bite her head off, but sounding too off-hand to be as uncaring as she wanted to appear, stayed her. And obviously assuming that she would be spending the weekend with her parents as Ashlie had previously suggested, Lynette asked, 'Will you be saying anything to your parents about me?'

Ashlie did not pretend not to know that she was asking if she would be telling them about her and Chase Marriner. But that Lynette seemed to care that her in-laws should not know, gave her spirits a lift, for surely that had to mean that she still felt a great deal for Norris.

'No,' she said, and left it at that.

But when everything she intended to take with her was neatly folded into her weekend case, she was suddenly struck by the humour of the situation. Here was she in her room packing to go away with Chase Marriner, while Lynette was in her room, doing the self-same thing! I'm getting hysterical, she thought, and no wonder.

Humour was to abruptly leave though when she thought of how Lynette would learn, when she went to her office the next day, that she would be unpacking that same suitcase tomorrow not in Paris as she expected, but exactly where she was now.

Her sense of humour had still not returned the following morning when she observed the look of anticipation in her sister-in-law's eyes.

'I'll see you some time on Monday evening,' said Lynette when, with her briefcase in one hand, and her weekend case in the other, she prepared to leave the flat. 'I expect you'll be coming back on Sunday won't you?' she thought to ask. 'Or were you thinking of making a crack-of-dawn start from Whittledene on Monday and going straight to work from there?'

'I'll see how things go,' Ashlie muttered, sounding not very forthcoming, she had to own. Though she was now herself a little panicky when Lynette, all too plainly on top of the world, thought to tease.

'Regretting that you promised to leave London for the weekend?'

'I don't know what you mean,' she answered, wondering if her inner turbulence was showing.

'Well, he must have that something extra to keep you out as late as you stayed out the other night—or should I say morning,' opined Lynette, still teasing.

'Oh, him,' she said, only just remembering that she had rung Lynette to say she had a date after work when she had gone to sit in wait for Chase Marriner on Wednesday. 'I wouldn't mind if I never saw him again.'

Lynette stayed only to give her a look that said with her staying out so late, who was she trying to kid, and

went off happily, to leave Ashlie hoping that Chase
Marriner would let her sister-in-law down lightly. She
had grown fond of her, and did not want her to be
hurt.

At lunch time Ashlie went along to her bank to
collect her francs, the thought with her that Chase
Marriner would surely have told Lynette by now.
Fleetingly it crossed her mind to keep well clear of
Hertfordshire that night. She had no idea what Chase
Marriner would do if she did not show up. Since he
must rate as the biggest smoothie of all time—quickly
she ousted the memory of what he had done to her
senses when his strong arms had come round her—she
saw that, if he had cut off his nose where Lynette was
concerned this weekend, that while, as yet, she had
done nothing by way of tricking him into keeping his
promise, that there was always next weekend, or the
weekend after for him to have Lynette in spite of any
bruised feelings.

Resigned by the time the afternoon came to a close
that she didn't know when next she would know
another moment's peace, Ashlie was just putting the
cover on her typewriter when her friend and fellow
secretary, Gillian Rogers, appeared, to walk to the car
park with her.

'I was going to suggest the cinema tonight,' said
Gillian as they left the building, 'but I spotted your
case in your car at lunch time. Going somewhere
nice?'

'Er—to my parents,' Ashlie replied, hoping she
wouldn't be called on to tell many more lies before this
whole business was over.

'They live in Lincolnshire, don't they?' Gillian
remembered. And at her confirmation, 'Take care—
snow is forecast for that area this weekend.'

She would take care all right, Ashlie thought, as she set off. Though since she wouldn't be driving anywhere near Lincolnshire, and with her parents not there but somewhere on the Welsh coast, the weather could do what it liked.

A wrinkle of worry touched her brow when turning her car into the drive of Clarendon House. It suddenly hit her that so unused was she to this underhand business, that she just had not given thought to the fact that when she landed back on English soil, her car would still be in the drive of Chase Marriner's home. Though, when she considered the tough time she stood to have in front of her, where she left her car, seemed to be the least of her troubles.

Taking her last breaths of freedom for a while, Ashlie collected her case from the back seat of her car, to present herself at the front door, and to ring the bell.

Her first surprise came in that it was not Chase Marriner who answered her ring, but the owner of the motherly voice she had spoken with on the telephone. She was a woman in her mid-sixties whose plump person was covered by a blue checked overall, and whom Ashlie thought must be his housekeeper.

'Oh—good evening,' she said, rapidly collecting herself. 'I'm Ashlie Holman.' Her name meant nothing, she saw, because for all the smiling lady maintained her smile, she did not step back to let her through the door. And it was left to Ashlie to give the information, 'Mr Marriner is expecting me.'

She saw his housekeeper glance to her case, and felt warm colour rise at the obvious construction there for her to read. Either she was used to opening the door on a Friday night to find some female looking ready to move in, or she was well schooled in not letting that smile slip. For that smile was still in place when Ashlie, listening for footsteps which would tell her that Chase Marriner was coming to relieve the embarrassment she was feeling, crossed through the doorway.

But there was no sound of footsteps. Nor, was she to discover, was there going to be any sign of him. For barely had the housekeeper got the front door closed, than she was saying:

'Mr Marriner is at the airport, but . . .'

'*Airport!*' Astounded, hardly crediting her hearing, Ashlie just gaped.

But the housekeeper, plainly a type who, herself unshockable—and living under Chase Marriner's roof as she did, that didn't surprise Ashlie—was quite able to recognise, and deal with, shock in others when she saw it. For, all before Ashlie had recovered from knowing that when she had been going to pull a fast one on Chase Marriner, that diabolical swine had pulled a fast one on her, she found she had been ushered to take a seat in the drawing room while the housekeeper went to make her a 'nice cup of tea'.

Like a fool, she had let herself be taken in to believe that—*that* libertine—had opted for her in place of Lynette, when all the time he'd had no intention of cancelling his arrangements with Lynette. Right at this very moment the two of them were probably going through passport control. Ashlie surfaced to go from being absolutely astounded, to be absolutely furious.

For the best part of the next two minutes, she thought of every vile name she could for him—and that still did not cover what she thought of him. Then, unable to bear being inside his house for another moment, she shot from her chair.

But, as she raced towards the door, and swung it wide to charge through it, Ashlie cannoned into someone just about to enter the room from the other side.

Strong arms were suddenly holding her steady. Strong, well-remembered arms, were about her as, receiving a fresh shock, she discovered she was looking up into the mocking face of none other than Chase Marriner.

'My oath,' he said, mockery not limited to his expression. 'You're as mad as hell about something, sweet Ashlie. Don't tell me Mrs Parry has upset you?'

His mocking tone as much as anything, put Ashlie on a more even keel. But when those arms seemed in no hurry to let go of her, she took a backward step out of his hold. His arms dropped to his sides. Ashlie took a further step back, her surprise showing in her voice.

'The lady who answered the door said you were at the airport!'

'The lady did not lie,' he replied. And silkily he added, 'Would you have preferred Lynette to be still waiting at the airport wondering where I'd got to?'

'You left it this late to tell her the weekend is off?' she exclaimed sharply, shaken again by his callousness. But she was to realise that there had been method in his callousness; his reply made her aware that they did not come much smarter than him.

'I should risk telling her while there was still time for you to practise a little double dealing?' he queried.

'I'm here, aren't I?' she said sourly.

'Under protest,' he replied, having, apparently, not one solitary illusion about her lack of enthusiasm. 'D'you think I don't know that if there was any way you could avoid being in my bed this weekend, that you'd take it?'

'If you know that, then I can't see why you agreed to start with,' she answered snappily, not made to feel any happier when he merely shrugged.

'You could say,' he paused to smile insincerely, 'I like a challenge.

Mrs Parry coming in with a tray of tea, saved her from having to think up a reply. And under cover of the housekeeper enquiring should she bring another cup, and Chase declining tea, Ashlie poured herself a cup and acknowledged that, as wise to her as Chase Marriner had revealed he was, it must be pure male egoism that had decided him to let go Lynette for her. That having seen that she had no stomach for this weekend, it had challenged the lady-killer in him to get her as clinging as the rest. That she had once clung to him in mindless response was not, by the look of it, sufficient.

Quickly she sent the alien memory of that single embrace on its way. But as Mrs Parry left the room, Ashlie knew agitation that her endeavours to save her brother's marriage might already be too late. For if he could so easily discard Lynette, then surely that had to mean that any challenge which Lynette presented, had already been met!

This, she was rapidly on to thinking, was not a moment to let good taste get in the way of what she wanted to know. A certainty was in her that this weekend was never going to get off the ground if the answer she received, to a question she should have asked before, was the wrong one.

'Tell me,' she started off abruptly, 'have you and Lynette already . . .' she faltered, the question getting stuck. But, sharp not the word for him, Chase, albeit with slightly raised eyebrows, had no objection to finishing for her.

'Been between the sheets?' Hating him afresh for his mockery, stubbornly, she wouldn't look away. But she had her answer, when, mockery fading, coolly, he told her, 'It would appear—by giving you my word—that I have, forever, denied myself that pleasure.'

'Which means you haven't?' The tremendous relief that rushed in was all too soon being countered by a sinking of spirits to know that, still in time to save Norris having cause to reject Lynette, she must go through with it—as far as Paris anyway.

'Not—yet,' Chase thought to qualify, his threat graphic, no need there for him to spell it out.

Hot and bothered that, from his threat, she could bank on him creating blue murder when in Paris she told him 'You backed the wrong filly' Ashlie thought a change of conversation was called for.

'You could have saved yourself a return journey to the airport,' she hurried to tell him. 'I could as easily have driven there, as here.'

'You fancy a look around an airport?' he enquired, being deliberately obtuse, she thought, just for the hell of it.

But, doing her best not to be goaded, patiently, she explained, 'What I meant was, that with you and I taking off for Paris—obviously on a later flight than the one you were going to take with Lynette—that I could have . . .'

'We're not going to France.'

She had forgotten that she still held her emptied cup, and saucer. But the rattle of china as his blunt statement shook her, had her hastily setting them down.

'We're—not going . . . You're saying that . . .' panic of a different sort took her, 'that you're calling the weekend off!'

He took his time in replying, deliberately studying her for long moments. Then slowly, he shook his head. 'Would I—when you've put in so much hard spade work?' he asked, to give her the definite feeling that he was tormenting her just for the pure hell of it. 'How can you think me such a cad,' he drawled, 'that I'd take you to the same location I had planned for my other—licentious—affair?'

'You're that sensitive!' she scorned, having had just about enough of him before they got started.

His reply was to grin, her barb not so much as touching him. But her flare of anger was to rapidly fizzle to nothing when, with a glance to her empty cup, he did no more than cross the room to take up her case, and to have her insides acting up, when pleasantly, he spoke.

'If you'd like to come with me, I'll show you upstairs.' And not making her feel any better that since she had arrived straight from her office he thought her begrimed by her day's toil. 'You may wish to freshen up before dinner,' he suggested.

Many times she had pictured the scene, but this wasn't the way it was supposed to go! Trying her best to hold down panic that Chase Marriner was all set to show her the way to his room, he had strolled with her case to the door before, on her feet, she found her voice to ask:

'W-we're staying—here?'

At the door, he turned. 'You have some objection?' he enquired mockingly, plainly not believing she was in any position to raise the smallest objection.

Ashlie had just about had her fill of him, his mockery, and the whole sorry business. She was heartily wishing that her brother had never met and married Lynette. Though, when it was touch and go that she would not lose her temper and go storming past him and out to the car, suddenly, flashing through her mind came the memory of Norris, oh so happy on his wedding day, his love for Lynette there for all to see, his eyes only for his beautiful bride at his side.

'It wasn't what we agreed,' she found herself staying to argue. 'I agreed to go away with you for the weekend, not to stay here in your home.'

She had heard Chase blunt before. He was blunt again when, not moving from the door, he questioned, 'Are you saying—no weekend away—no bed?'

That he had gone to sound arrogant, was no improvement on mockery. But though she could tell that as far as he was concerned, which bed, or where that bed was located, was highly immaterial, she could also perceive from his arrogance that any minute now might see him throwing in the towel and telling her that he had gone off the idea of bedding her. And as her stomach started to churn, she lost sight entirely of what this new development would do to her plan to trick him, though found instead that the stubbornness she was having to learn to live with, was refusing to let her back down.

'That's—what I'm saying,' she replied, wondering if in some Freudian fashion she was begging him to show her the door.

But when tensely she waited to know which it was to be, she found that she was too numb to know what to make of his muttered, 'Another plan misfired.' She still had not moved when, 'Either I take you away now, and upset Mrs Parry by letting her culinary efforts go to waste,' he weighed the situation up, 'or, I spend this night solitary in my bed.' Her nerve ends starting to fray, Ashlie was still no clearer what was to happen when, in a tone there was just no arguing with, shortly, he commanded, 'Follow me.'

Awareness came through her numbed feelings then, that having come to a decision, Chase Marriner would stick to it. And that, should it be to the front door he escorted her, she would be wasting her time in trying to get him to change his mind.

CHAPTER FOUR

HER heart thudding painfully, Ashlie followed Chase Marriner out into the hall. In front lay the wide outside door, and, her courage having got her this far was now suddenly used up. She just did not know what she was going to do if he kept on walking towards that door.

But she was not to be in suspense for long. When they reached the point where a simple left turn would take them to the elegant staircase, he halted, and she felt his hand come beneath her elbow, and it was in that direction that he turned her.

To climb the staircase with him was not conducive to any lessening of her heavy heart beats, and all her senses were alert for any sudden move he might make. But she was to breathe a fraction more normally when he took her to the far end of the landing, and opened up what she saw was nothing more than a linen store.

'Mrs Parry will be busy preparing a meal,' he remarked suavely, his observant eyes taking in his now silent companion before he piled bed linen and fluffy towels into her arms, then said, sarcastically she thought, 'You won't mind making your own bed, I'm sure.'

'Anything to help Mrs Parry,' she murmured, and saw his lips twitch that having found her tongue, she was trying out a little sarcasm of her own. She guessed then that there was little that went on in her head that Chase did not have some clue to.

But, awash with relief that, this night at any rate, it

looked as though she was going to sleep as solitarily in her bed as he was in his, Ashlie carrying her linen, followed her pillows-and-blanket-carrying host back down along the landing, until he stopped at one of the doors.

It was this door he opened. She followed him in, her eyes noting the tasteful furnishings while at the same time she watched him dump the bedding he was carrying down into one of the bedroom chairs.

'Dinner will be ready in about fifteen minutes,' he advised as he turned to face her. And his eyes lingering for a suggestive second on her mouth, 'I'll leave you to come down when you're ready.'

The moment he had gone Ashlie sank down to the edge of the bed. She felt as though she had just crossed some treacherous minefield—and this was only the beginning! Oh God, what had she done?

Seconds, and then minutes began to tick away as she gathered her second wind, but could still see nothing for it but, that, she would have to go the rest of the course. What else could she do? Chase had agreed to leave Lynette alone, but only if she spent a few nights away with him. So if she backed out now, as every instinct urged, then she would have broken her word, and, without question, he would feel under no obligation about cancelling his word to her.

Committed, as she saw it, to going on with it if she was to get him to keep his word, Ashlie saw, there being nothing else she could do, that when the morrow came, she was going to have to play it by ear. In the meantime, her heartfelt thanks went to the respect he had for his housekeeper's labours in the kitchen. For tonight at least, she had, via Mrs Parry, earned a reprieve.

Drawing a blank when it came to trying to think up

some way of earning a reprieve for tomorrow night, and—since Lynette had not been going to return until Monday—Sunday night too, Ashlie moved and quickly made up the bed before panic could have another go at her. Hurriedly too, she washed, reapplied her light make-up, then ran a comb through her short wavy hair. And having gone to work that day in a newish suit, she straightened her skirt, and not wanting him to come looking for her, she left her room to go down to the only other room she knew in the house.

It was there that she found Chase. He had changed his business suit for casual slacks and a sweater, and was in conversation with his housekeeper.

'You're here at last, Ashlie,' he said when he saw her, a world of charm about him as she came further into the room. 'Miss Holman will be staying the night,' he turned to inform Mrs Parry, charm still there, though Ashlie did not miss his sarcasm when, as an afterthought, he added, 'Though Miss Holman was pleased to make up a bed for herself—weren't you Ashlie?'

'I could have done that,' protested Mrs Parry, before Ashlie could find an answer that would show him that sarcasm was not his right alone.

'It was no trouble,' Ashlie smiled, and had no need to add anything more as with that same charm, her host escorted her to the dining room, remarking that he hoped she was hungry enough to do justice to the meal.

While having to admit that his manners were impeccable in front of his housekeeper, Ashlie was of the certain opinion that all that would change when Mrs Parry left them. But, once they were seated and by themselves, she was pleasantly surprised to discover that Chase had not one mocking or suggestive remark to make as they disposed of a pâté starter.

They were on the second course when, able to converse easily on any subject, not the smallest barbed comment had fallen from his lips. But it was only when she realised that, with him keeping well away from personalities, he had so far lulled her away from what had seemed an ever present anxiety state, and she was actually *smiling* in amusement at something he had just said, that her smile quickly departed. She was then to bring herself up short to mentally repeat over and over; a rake, is a rake, is a rake.

They were at the dessert stage when a frown touched her brow that for the last ten minutes it had been uphill work to remember 'a rake, is a rake, is a rake' and she discovered that the meal was not going to be completed without personalities coming up for discussion.

But though on her guard, as she wondered if he had deliberately set out to put her at her ease before he got her to talk about herself, Ashlie could see no reason to avoid answering his question of what work did she do. She might, she mused, even get the chance to appeal to any sense of decency buried deep down inside him.

'I work as a secretary for Middleton's, the lifting gear manufacturers,' she replied pleasantly.

'You enjoy your work?'

'It's quite interesting,' she replied, her mind set to get in a plug for Norris and Lynette if she could. 'Though I've only been with the firm about six months.'

'You believe in changing employers frequently?' Chase enquired, a hint of a smile about his mouth as he drew her out.

Ashlie shook her head. 'Up until a year ago, I was

with the same firm I went to when I left school.' She smiled to cover how emotionally disastrous it had been when, deciding she was getting in a rut, she had left her nice safe job and had gone to work for Kevan Salter.

'You then felt like a change?' he asked, that hint of a smile still there as his eyes flicked to the curve of her mouth.

'That's right,' she replied, holding her smile as she went on, 'But that job didn't last long. I was living with my parents in a small town in Lincolnshire at the time. But when Norris married Lynette and then had to honour the contract he'd signed for a two-year stint in Brazil, Lynette missed him so much that she asked me to come and move in with her.'

Quite pleased with her plug, her smile was to slip and fade altogether when choosing to ignore completely that she had just introduced her brother and his marriage into the conversation, Chase remarked thoughtfully,

'So, before you were fully established in your new job, you decided to throw it up.' And to show that when it came to reading in between the lines he was a passed master he quietly asked, 'What happened back there in Lincolnshire?'

'What do you mean, what happened?' she asked shortly, starting to get annoyed. It only took the shrewd glint that was suddenly there in his eyes, to tell her that her short sharp answer had him aware that she had some reason for not wanting to discuss it. Though that did not stop him from pressing to hear more.

'Something must have happened,' he calmly replied. 'Or why not only resign? But to leave your home too?'

Insensitive brute, Ashlie thought. He had another think coming if he thought he'd get an answer.

Though her stubbornness not to reply was prodded that it did sound a trifle goody-goody that, with no more reason than that Lynette was lonely, she had thrown up her job in order to keep her company.

'There were other circumstances, which helped me to make up my mind,' she admitted coldly.

If she had thought that should he possess even the *smallest* sensitivity, that he would accept from her prim cold manner that she had no wish to say more, then she was to learn that Chase Marriner was about as sensitive as a plank.

For he was not the least put off in his quest to know all there was to know, as, mockery once more appeared. 'Ah,' he said, drawing her anger as she guessed he had just added two and two to make four. 'Enter the dastardly philanderer,' he drawled sardonically. The look of dislike she threw him left him unmoved.

She drew in a tight breath, and suppressed an almost overwhelming urge to thump him. Not only had he hit the nail on the head, but it hurt that her suffering at that time should be referred to so lightly.

'I've had my baptism of fire with *your* sort,' she said acidly.

'And ran away,' he murmured, something, as her barb glanced off him, which she guessed he would never do—not until he'd had his full retribution. But, 'Tell me,' he went on to enquire easily, 'did you run before—or after—you got burned?'

She was not entirely sure what it was he was asking. But if he was asking had she had an affair in the full sense of the word, then he could go and run for his answer. Though, on the point of letting him run for his answer anyway, Ashlie suddenly saw a golden opportunity to knock him off his arrogant perch.

'Like Lynette, it was my boss I fell for, and put up there on a pedestal. But, as Lynette discovered at the airport tonight, the males we make gods of, too frequently turn out to have feet of clay.'

Again her poison tipped spear did not touch him. He even smiled as though to suggest that—feet of clay or no—if the agreement she had made with him wasn't carried out to the letter, then Lynette would still be his.

But, her anxieties became once more a crushing weight, when he still had sufficient gall to enquire, 'Does it still hurt—discovering your god was merely mortal?'

Ashlie found it impossible to sit fencing words with him any longer. Her answer was to get to her feet. 'I've had a busy day,' she said as politely as she could, 'I'm sure you'll excuse me if I go to my room.'

Why she waited that extra second or two, Ashlie never knew. But, perhaps waiting for some caustic reply by way of a good night, pause she did, her chin tilted that fraction higher—a feature not missed by the man who sat studying her mutinous expression.

But, having waited long enough for any rejoinder, polite or otherwise, Ashlie moved. 'Good night,' she said, and went quickly to the door.

'Ashlie.'

Chase saying her name halted her when she had been ready to turn the door handle. She turned round, but as far as she was concerned, any sarcastic parting shot he had to offer, could be heard from where she stood. She did not care at all for the sudden wicked light that was there in his eyes. And she definitely did not care at all for the silkily drawled words that left him, when, after several more moments of his eyes taking his fill, softly, he spoke.

'My—lady friends—usually kiss me good night—*at least.*'

Ashlie made an instinctive movement to turn to face the door, but came to her senses and realised she would be pushing it if she followed her instinct and went sailing out of the room. She had made an agreement with him, and any welshing on that agreement would render all she had been through to get this far, a waste of time.

But it was only by telling herself that if the *most* he would be demanding that night was a good night kiss, then she was still getting off very lightly, that she felt sure enough to leave her position by the door.

Wary that the moment she got near him he might take it into his head to make a grab for her, she halted only when she was close up to his chair. But when he made no move to touch her, she was to feel inadequate to know what to do, until, impatient with herself, she bent her head.

His mouth beneath hers was warm, and was inviting a deeper kiss, and Ashlie was suddenly beginning to tingle all over. All at once she was discovering, when Chase was making not the slightest move to grab hold of her or so much as lay a finger on her, the most contradictory feeling of wanting her mouth to stay over his until she did get some response from him.

Abruptly, she pulled back. 'Good night,' she repeated and, with her cheeks starting to burn with the thought that just from the feel of his lips against hers—and no help from him—she had wanted more, Ashlie fled.

She was still wondering about that oddest of odd effects the feel of Chase Marriner's mouth against hers had brought, when washed and changed into her mini nightshirt, she climbed into bed. But, finding no answer for why her insides should act up the way they had, Ashlie then changed her thoughts' direction, to wonder about him.

His reaction, or more precisely, lack of reaction, she found a trifle non-plussing. Kevan Salter now, would never have let an opportunity like that go by. Kevan would but definitely have made that grab for her which she had been expecting Chase to make.

Which all went to prove, she was having to face some minutes later, that, deeply dyed philanderers both, where Kevan sniffed around all females as though they were bitches in season, Chase had far more finesse.

Accepting that he had a more mature outlook than Kevan, she was then to recall how Chase had said he liked a challenge. It was only then that she began to see that it wasn't that her appeal was greater than Lynette's or that she wore the dubious title of 'chosen one' but purely that since Chase had seen that she would take any way she could find to not be in his bed, she represented more of a challenge than her sister-in-law.

At that point, Ashlie realised her thinking was starting to grow confused. For surely, Chase was a man who would take up that challenge at the first opportunity—that opportunity presented to him when, downstairs, she had kissed him.

A minute later she had seen how truly a man of his word he was. For, remembering how she had stuck out that 'the weekend' did not begin until he had taken her away, it was she who had had to kiss him, and he, had left it at that!

But, realising that she was on the way to admiring something in him; that he was to be trusted, that he was not the grab-whenever-the-chance-arose type, her

heart was to suddenly start pounding. And she was to
wonder when she heard sounds that told her the
master was retiring for the night, and that he was on
his way upstairs, if she was not just a naïve idiot to
trust his word.

A tense bundle of nerves all at once, Ashlie held her
breath as those footsteps approached. She was not
breathing at all when those footsteps halted, right
outside her door!

Having received a scare that made her wonder what
the dickens she would be like tomorrow night when,
away, their agreement would come into force, she only
began to breathe normally again when the footsteps
moved on, and she heard the sound of another door
open, and then close.

To her surprise, when she had thought with so
much to worry her that she would never sleep, Ashlie
slept well that night, though she was to awaken early
to a pale grey day. With those many worries
immediately there to ferret away at her, there was not
the remotest chance that she would be able to get back
to sleep again.

In no hurry to start what she knew in advance was
going to be the most tricky day of her life, Ashlie lay
where she was. This day would start soon enough
without her leaping out of bed to meet it.

Though when her imagination began to get out of
hand when she visualised Chase Marriner refusing to
take no for an answer, she knew she was not aiding her
attempts to hold down panic, by simply lying there
and letting her imagination take over.

Quickly she left her bed, wanting with everything in
her to be away from Clarendon House. Momentarily
she wondered—dare she risk backing out? Dare she
run away and return to the flat in the hope of Lynette

being so angry and affronted when she told her how Chase Marriner had been all set to two-time her, that Lynette would give him the big 'E'?

The notion was scrapped. The memory of her sister-in-law openly saying that it didn't matter to her that he had other women, and that he could make her feel that other women did not exist, came to squash it.

Ashlie damned his hide and that smooth charm that apparently made no woman safe from him. But the fact still remained that she just did not dare to take that risk. She was going to have to go away with him, and somehow ensure that she slept as solitarily in her bed tonight, and tomorrow night, as she had slept last night.

Deeply involved with the awfulness of her situation, she had moved to stare unseeing out of the window without knowing it. Suddenly the quiet tranquil scene had begun to register.

It was the first time she had seen the gardens and fields that surrounded Clarendon House. The sight from her window of vales and hills charmed away her anxiety about the precariousness of her position. There had been a hard frost during the night, and the picture of garden shrubs and trees clad in tinselly silver ice, was enchanting.

For what seemed age-long minutes, she was to know peace and calm, her thoughts far away from the predicament she was in.

It was not to last. Suddenly a sound in her room penetrated, and she spun round. The enchantment still there in her eyes quickly faded when she saw that Chase Marriner had silently entered her room!

With hot colour rushing to her face, she barely noticed that he was holding a tray bearing a cup and saucer. She did notice though, that Chase was not yet dressed. And from what she could see of him that was not covered by his short towelling robe, it was obvious that robe was about the only thing he had on!

Transfixed, unable to move away from the window, she saw his eyes travel the length of her. Those grey eyes paused appreciatively at the amount of shapely thigh she was exposing. Unable to make any sort of trite remark, Ashlie was inwardly cursing the day she had ever thought a mini-nightshirt so terrific that she'd had to have one. For while the wrist length sleeves were more than decorous, the same could not be said for the length of the rest of the garment.

'I thought you might like to start the day off right,' said Chase, a warm look in his eyes she didn't care for, as he came further into her room.

Her eyes were still glued to the view beyond the window and she hoped with all her heart, when he placed the tray down, that his remark signified nothing other than he thought her day would start off right if she began it with a cup of tea.

'You shouldn't—have bothered,' she managed to murmur. Alarm was having a field day in her when he straightened from depositing the tray, and she saw he had taken another step closer.

'It was no bother,' he replied easily, that warm look now resting on her shiny tousled hair. 'Mrs Parry has a lie in at the weekends,' he commented pleasantly, his eyes transferring to her mouth. Ashlie was still eyeing him warily, when he added, 'I'll make a start on breakfast presently.'

That he was not above cooking his own breakfast, and hers too by the sound of it, was of little interest to her other than she wished that he would go and get on with it straight away. But having got over the first shock of him coming in and catching her in her ridiculous nightshirt, she tried for a sophistication she just did not own, as she endeavoured to hasten his departure.

'I'll just have a quick bath, then I'll come and help you,' she offered.

'I'd appreciate your—co-operation,' he replied, the devil-light that was suddenly dancing in his eyes enough to tell her that he had seen through her attempt to be as sophisticated as the rest of his women friends. It seemed too, he was deriving some enjoyment from tormenting her.

She ignored the meaning in his remark, though she hoped he would not ignore the large hint she intended in her, 'I'll run my bath while I drink my tea.' And then she wished him in hell when, with that malicious light still there in his eyes, his mouth picked up at the corners.

'Got a good morning kiss for me?' he asked.

Beginning to wonder if her heart would ever again know the same steady beat it had drummed to before she had known him, Ashlie was then set to consider how to get him from her room, and quickly. It might be the better option to kiss him than to stand—where he had too much of a view of her legs and thighs—fencing words with him. He had not made a grab for her last night when she had given him the kiss he'd requested, had he?

She had still not come to any decision when, by the simple expedient of moving forward and placing his hands on her arms, Chase took the choice of decision from her. And before her alarm had time to get started, his head was coming down, and his mouth was over hers.

Ashlie's heart beat wildly as she was drawn yet closer, so that with his lips still over hers she felt his body heat. She tried to draw back, and put her hands up to his chest to push him away.

But the push she attempted was to be puny as, when his kiss deepened, some other instinct took charge of her. And when he kissed her again, she forgot what she had put her hands against his chest for, and slid them up and over his shoulders.

When next Chase kissed her, she was not thinking at all. She had felt his body heat, and enjoyed that warmth. But found, when she pressed herself to him, that it was not merely a warmth from him that she felt, but fire, coming from within herself too.

Her heart gave an excited leap when his hands caressed her back through her nightshirt, and she was standing on tip toe the better to strain yet closer to him when his hands caressed down to her tiny waist.

Ashlie still had her arms up and over his shoulders, the material of her nightshirt riding up with her movement. She was mindless to all but the knowledge that never had she been kissed nor wanted to be kissed like this before.

One hand strayed to caress her left hip. Suddenly then, great strident bells of alarm went off in her head. For with Chase holding her close up to him with one hand, his other hand had continued its caressing downward movement to where her nightshirt had run out of material. And, shaken to the depths of her being, belated modesty then had her conscious that Chase was now pressing the lower half of her to him with the hand that now held captive a naked curve of her pert behind!

A gasp breaking from her, Ashlie drew her hands back down to his chest, and pushed, and meant it. But even as Chase let her go and stepped back, she could still feel the scorching imprint of the hand that had held her left buttock secure.

'I-I th-think—you'd better go,' she stammered, her nerve ends all of a jangle. But there was a huskiness in her voice when she added, 'I w-want to have a bath and get dressed.'

Chase made no attempt to take her back in his arms, but that he was still there with her gave her little cause for relief. That he knew full well what he had done to her, was all too apparent though, when his tone silky, he softly murmured to her,

'Are you sure you want to get dressed, Ashlie?'

She did not think she would be sure about anything ever again. But she needed desperately to be by herself. From somewhere she found sufficient wit to remind him,

'We—that is—our . . .' And having made a false stab at it, bluntly she got it out, 'You agreed that—the weekend doesn't start until—we're away.'

He took his time in answering her, but as, trying not to show her panic, Ashlie warily eyed him, she was to sense that, he was a man who loved a challenge and he had seen a challenge in what she had just said! Her panic was beginning to get the better of her. She had no idea if he would reply with some remark such as 'To hell with going away' when, his next move could be one to take her back in his arms, or if he would be content to take up that challenge some other time.

Praying, aware of her weakness, that he would remain the man of his word she had believed him, to Ashlie it seemed that a life time had elapsed with Chase saying nothing, and doing nothing, except to look at her with that very definite gleam of being ready to take up whatever challenge she offered.

Then all at once he moved to the door, and she felt ready to collapse, when she heard that mocking tone was back when from the door he drawled, 'Don't be late down to breakfast, sweet Ashlie.'

The strength in her legs went the moment the door closed behind him. Glad to find the bed so near, she collapsed upon it, her mind in a whirl at the added complication which she had just been forced to recognise.

The complication was staring her in the face to tell her that somehow, a man she hated, with whom she had planned to go away but had no intention of sleeping with, had the power to make her want to do just that! As much as she would like to hide from that fact in remembering how on fire for him she had felt when she had been in his arms, Ashlie could not deny that she had wanted Chase Marriner!

CHAPTER FIVE

To find Chase no longer robe-clad, but wearing slacks and a sweater similar to those he had worn last night, helped calm her shaken thinking when, Ashlie eventually joined him in the kitchen. He was disturbing enough without her seeing more evidence of the virile masculinity of his strong uncovered, hair-bedecked legs.

The memory of his hand warm and cupped over that naked part of her sprung unbidden to her and had her wordless as she took the place he indicated she should take at the kitchen table.

But another plus was waiting for her. For when she had nerve enough to look at him, she saw that the light of having picked up the gauntlet she had unconsciously thrown down, had gone from his eyes. And for an added bonus, she could hear no mockery there when, obviously in no hurry to be away, he suggested she should take her time with the first meal of the day, saying that he favoured a leisurely start.

'I expect you're always rushing from one place to another?' she said, thinking that maybe she should say something so long as the subject matter remained impersonal.

'Business life does have its stresses,' he agreed. 'Which is why, whenever I can, I like to take it easy at the weekends.'

Sensing dangerous ground, Ashlie replied noncommittally, 'I suppose that's why the weekend was invented.' And could almost have grown to like him—

but not quite—that he did not come back with any double-edged comment about this particular weekend.

It had gone nine o'clock by the time breakfast was over and Ashlie had returned to her room for her weekend case. Chase was then held up with taking a couple of phone calls. Though when they were on their way out and the phone shrieked for a third time, he ignored it. 'We won't get there before midnight at this rate,' he muttered, and ushered her out through the front door.

Ashlie's nerves again started to bite, and she only just managed to hold back from saying that she wouldn't mind if his whole day was spent on the phone if it meant they wouldn't get where they were heading at all.

But all too soon she was sitting beside him, the car in motion, and she knew that this was it—the weekend away had begun.

Feeling numbed, Ashlie was silent for the first hour of the journey. Then it broke through her numbness that, since Chase had no comment to make either, he must be the kind of driver who preferred his passengers to sit quiet and not to rattle on.

But having come round to some awareness, even the silence became a strain. So whether he wanted a non-rattling passenger or not, Ashlie suddenly asked in a rush.

'We're not going by motorway? I've noticed,' she said more slowly, the observation just coming to her, 'that we seem to be travelling on minor roads.'

'You appeared to appreciate the view from your bedroom window,' Chase replied. 'I thought you might have an eye for countryside beauty.'

Surprised, that for all it was a grey day, he had chosen the more scenic route solely for her benefit,

Ashlie discovered an interest in their destination she had thought not to have.

'I didn't ask,' she said. She then pondered if her chances of having a room to herself at their journey's end would be better or worse, if instead of kicking all the way she tried to be an amenable companion. 'Where are we making for?'

'I thought the Yorkshire Dales might appeal,' he replied pleasantly enough. 'But if . . .'

'The Dales sound fine,' said Ashlie, surprised again that it was not purely his own pleasure he had in mind. For to complete their agreement that he had to take her away at all, a weekend spent in the next town would still have constituted taking her away.

It confused her somewhat, that having caught her delighting in the view at his home, he had for *her* pleasure decided not only on a countryside route which would mean hours of driving for him, but he had also chosen to take her to an area which she knew, from childhood visits there with her parents, held some of the most beautiful country.

But that thought, in turn, brought Ashlie *dis*pleasure. Because in recalling those childhood trips to the Dales with her parents, and the happiness they had brought, she knew for certain that whether this trip went the way she wanted it to go or not, she would never again associate the Dales with happy childhood memories.

'My parents used to sometimes take me to the Dales when I was small,' she rallied to tell him then. 'And Norris too,' she added, peeved enough with her thoughts to want to have a go at him if she could. All thoughts of trying out the amenable tack had gone from her. 'We all loved it,' she said, and for good measure, 'Norris particularly.'

Talk about falling on stony ground! she thought crossly. For Chase Marriner expressed not the smallest interest in Norris, or what fun they'd had on their visits to their neighbouring county of Yorkshire. Instead, he asked a most off-putting question.

'Your parents are happily married?'

Taken out of her stride, it was a moment before she could move away from her attempts to push Lynette's husband to the forefront of his mind.

'Very happily married,' she replied then. 'They're as happy now as the day they were married, and they've been married a long time since Norris is thirty-four now.' She was about to press on, the words already there on her lips, that so long as one Chase Marriner kept his amorous nose out of it, she was sure that Lynette and Norris would be as equally happily married as her parents. But oddly Ashlie found she was not saying that at all. Some element of curiosity side tracked her, and compelled her to say, 'How about you. Are your parents happy in their marriage?'

'They're happy,' he shrugged, his eyes leaving the road to flick a glance in her direction, 'but only because they're no longer married to each other.'

'They're divorced?'

His eyes were back on the road in front, but as she looked at him she saw him nod. Ashlie was left to guess from the little he had said that his parents wedded bliss constituted one long and continuous cat and dog fight. She found her curiosity was still at work, a curiosity which she would not have thought to have in relation to him.

'Is that why you've never married?' she asked.

She caught his grin, but was glad to note his mockery was absent still, when, 'Nope,' he said, adding, 'and don't try dreaming up any psychological problems, which I promise you just don't exist, for my remaining a bachelor. My formative years,' he went on easily, to tell her, 'were spent at boarding school—when I did go home—my sparring parents were hardly ever there.'

From that she guessed that, come the school holidays, Chase had been handed over to the Marriners housekeeper for her to look after. And recalling the consideration Chase gave to Mrs Parry, she saw that it was no wonder he had such a great respect for housekeepers in general.

'Were—you aware as a child, that your parents marriage was not a happy one?' she asked.

'Aware—certainly,' he answered, not taking exception to her curiosity. 'They'd always gone their separate ways. It was no hard shock when my father told me it was over.'

Why she should feel something akin to sympathy that, from the sound of it, his home life with his parents had been distinctly chilly, Ashlie could not have said. Certainly the type of man he had grown into neither deserved nor needed, anyone's sympathy. But she could not deny feeling a most unwanted pang of pity that when she realised, in the light of her own childhood being so love filled, Chase must have had a wretched time of it. It caused her voice to soften when, unable to hold the question back, she asked quietly,

'Have you ever known the warmth of love?'

Her sympathy, her fellow feeling, was not needed she was soon to find. Mockery had obviously reared its ugly head, when, deliberately misreading her question, Chase enquired sarcastically,

'Did it do you any good?'

'I wasn't prying into—for the want of a better

description—your *love* life,' Ashlie snapped, berating herself for being the biggest idiot of all time that, for a moment, it should affect her whatever sort of a childhood had been his lot. 'I merely wondered about your parents, and if . . .' Suddenly she realised her questions were completely lacking in sensitivity. Even as she blamed the totally loveless way Chase Marriner proposed to make her his for the lack of her normal sensitivity, still, she could not finish what she had begun to ask.

But not so he. 'You're wondering if there was love in that house at all?' he finished for her, the words 'that house' telling her that love had not been present, before he carelessly tacked on, 'What you never have, you never miss.'

Silence reigned once more. Then Ashlie was telling herself that they had to talk about something! She wondered about that curiosity about him that had so perplexingly surfaced within her. Then found that since her previous questions had not offended him in the smallest degree, she could not resist asking another one.

'Has the lack of love in your home, the fact that your parents didn't get on, been instrumental in making you think you can do without marriage?' she asked, and clarified what she was asking, by enquiring further, without quite knowing why she had got started on this anyway, 'I mean, did you make some conscious decision not to marry because you know that any marriage you made would be bound to end in divorce too?'

Chase negotiated the car round a small hazard up in front, and then Ashlie again had evidence that he was not taking exception to her allowing her curiosity verbal freedom. She saw the corner of his mouth pick up as though he found her questions amusing, then lightly, he remarked:

'You're at it again.'

'Prying?' she queried, though without heat since prying she had to own, was, in this instance, exactly what she had been doing. But it was not prying of which Chase was accusing her, she was to find.

'Psychoanalysing,' he murmured. And when she had thought he was going to leave it there and that it was her turn to whistle for an answer, he was adding, 'Though your theory is quite interesting.' Mockingly then, when she had thought him to be giving serious consideration to what he called her theory, he went on, 'I confess myself intrigued to know more. For instance, why, in your valued opinion—should I ever so far forget the joys I find in the freedom of bachelorhood and tie myself down—would any marriage I entered into, end in divorce?'

His sarcastic 'in your valued opinion' had stung and Ashlie found herself wishing she had never put her question. And it stung her too, that for all he had not appeared offended, he was clearly telling her to mind her own business.

'It's a foregone conclusion, isn't it?' she retorted. 'It goes without saying that no one woman would be enough for you and that, should any woman ever be sufficiently daft to want to exchange wedding vows with you, then she'd soon find herself alone nights while you went hunting in pastures new.' That, she thought irritably, should put paid to his mockery.

But no. It was still there when he murmured, 'Well thank God I'm not the marrying type.' Pleasantly, he added, 'Though you've obviously never heard that reformed—er—rakes, make the best husbands.'

'I shouldn't like to put that to the test,' said Ashlie

waspishly, and was back to wanting to thump him when, annoyingly, he drawled,

'Rest easy, sweet Ashlie. It's a test you won't have to fear from me.'

That he had as good as told her that she need have no fear that he would ever ask her to marry him, had her silently railing against him and she was un-communicative for the next stretch of their journey—not that he appeared to notice.

But by the time Chase was pulling the car to a stop outside an old coaching house, telling her that they would break there for lunch, Ashlie had started to see that she had taken his remark, personal though it had been, far too seriously. For, should the day ever dawn that 'Rake' Marriner ever so far forgot himself to ask her to marry him—not that he'd get the chance because once this weekend was over she would take jolly good care not to come within a mile of his orbit ever again—then wouldn't she have something sweet and choice to say in answer.

He came round and courteously opened the passenger door for her, and in getting out she flicked a glance to his face, good looking still for all it was now set in stern lines. All at once, and against all preconceived notion, she discovered that she did not want to be bad friends with him, and that she wanted him to be looking good humoured again. And so it was when, not stopping to think it would be much better for him to remain a stern-faced companion if it meant he was coming away from the idea of having her in his bed, that Ashlie found herself offering him a smile.

Quickly then when she observed his steady stare at this smiling change in her from the solemn, almost morose, companion she had been this last hour, Ashlie looked down. But his, 'Good,' had her raising her eyes enquiringly, her heart giving a giddy and unexpected leap when she saw that by some miracle her smile had worked, in that the good-humoured look was back in his expression again.

'Good?' she queried.

'At last you've stopped sulking,' he offered cheerfully.

'Oh—button it!' she said crossly, and knew the strain of it all must be proving too much and that she must be going potty. For when Chase burst out laughing at being, in effect, rudely told to 'shut up' by the tall slender girl by his side, as he caught hold of her elbow and headed her towards the coaching house, had her life depended upon it, Ashlie could not keep from joining in.

Whether it was because the meal they had stopped for had begun with laughter, or whether the fact that being among other people was conducive to make her feel relaxed, she did not know. But when occasionally throughout the meal Chase made some comment that had her smile peeping through again, she was to realise that mere charm did not begin to cover what Chase Marriner had going for him.

That some of her answers or remarks alternately amused him and sometimes had him looking at her as if he found her an enjoyable person to lunch with could, she thought, be all part and parcel of his highly potent charm. She certainly had to admit that her feeling of euphoria had little to do with the glass of wine she had taken with her meal when, lunch over, Chase stood back to allow her to go before him and, admiration in his eyes, he asked:

'Did you go into the hairdresser's with your hair that fantastic colour?'

'Believe it,' she murmured, and went in front of him to the door, where they parted when she went to hunt for the ladies room.

It was the pink flush that still tinged her cheeks as she looked into the mirror to repair her lipstick, that was to have Ashlie hitting the earth with a bump.

Oh God, no, she inwardly groaned. She had been through this whole disaster of taking a fall for a man of his type before. It couldn't be happening again. It just couldn't!

Ten minutes later, having given herself the most severest talking to, Ashlie left the ladies room; and by then she was of the opinion that she had panicked needlessly. Admittedly, Chase Marriner's charm was heady stuff, but, having once been inoculated against men like him, she was again confident that she was immune.

Just the same, it suited her quite well that when once more she sat beside him and again on the road, Chase appeared not to want to talk to her, and seemed to be as silently preoccupied with his thoughts, as she was with hers. For her part, she was again sternly reminding herself that not one tiny scrap of encouragement was she going to give him.

The day that had started out overcast was still grey when, some time around four that afternoon, Chase drove into a smart-looking country hotel. It was then that panic started to grip Ashlie in earnest. They had arrived!

She had never been away for the weekend, or during the week for that matter, for the purpose for which this weekend had been planned. She was engulfed by embarrassment when, with her car coat over her arm, both their cases down by her feet, she stood away from the reception desk and left Chase to fill in their registration cards. She was certain that everyone knew what they were there for.

Positive that her face was scarlet, she looked at neither Chase nor the hotel porter when the three of them travelled up in the lift, and the porter then led the way to their room.

Her nerves were stretched and threatening to snap. She was too strung up to experience even minimal comfort from the fact that it was not solely a bedroom to which they had been shown, but a suite that consisted of a small sitting room, a bedroom, bathroom and tiny kitchenette.

She was aware vaguely of the porter carrying their cases through to the bedroom, though what words passed between Chase and him before the porter pocketed his tip and departed, she was too busy dealing with panic to comprehend.

When Chase came into the sitting room from his inspection of their accommodation, Ashlie had not moved. Though move she did when he stretched out a hand to touch her. As she instinctively jerked from him, she saw, too late, that he had merely been going to remove a piece of fluff from her sleeve, and had not been making a 'we're away now—so let's get on with it' grab for her. But her movement of rejection angered him, and she got that message loud and clear when, in no mood to keep his anger to himself, Chase let rip.

'For God's sake, we've only just got here!' he fairly bellowed, a tight look about his well-shaped mouth. 'It might be usual for your other *libertine* friends to tear your clothes from you the moment they have you anywhere near a bed, but right at this moment, a shower and some refreshment have more appeal than you.'

What she might have answered, Ashlie didn't have time to discover. For whether her enraged escort preferred a shower or not, it was not to the bathroom that he went, but slamming out from the suite.

Anger was to visit her too then, and she was careless that he had furiously taken himself off. As far as she was concerned, she hoped he never came back. Who the hell did he think he was anyway? Where did he get off telling her that right at this moment she held no appeal for him? They both knew what they were there for! Did he expect her to pretend that she didn't? All that rubbish about wanting a shower and some refreshment! She'd like to bet that if she had stayed still while he de-fluffed her sleeve, that he would have not been content to so readily take his hands from her—the arrogant licentious swine.

Having worked herself up into a fine fury against him, her anger plummeted when, answering a discreet tap on the door, she saw a porter standing there holding a tray of tea for two.

'Thank you,' she murmured, standing aside while the porter came in and placed the tray down.

So Chase did have some refreshment in mind, she thought wearily, all anger gone. Feeling mentally drained, and suddenly, physically worn, even though she had done little but sit in the car all day, Ashlie ambled about the suite until, in the bedroom, she took advantage of Chase's absence and, slipping off her shoes, she stretched out on top of the bed.

Still desperately hoping that her only experience of the bed was going to be this small rest to re-new both her mental and physical strengths; Ashlie was sure that with Chase so mad with her he had put from him all thoughts of a shower and a cup of tea, that he had taken himself off for a walk.

He had been so angry he was unlikely to come back in a hurry, so she put her mind to wonder what excuses she could use for when he did return. Her memory of books she'd read, and of television plays she'd seen, told her that the headache plea had been overdone. But, without a blemish on her skin, she couldn't see how she would get away with a sudden attack of some contagious disease such as measles.

Ashlie was on her way to wondering, when she had the slenderest of ankles, if a plea of a sprained ankle would wash, when her eyelids began to droop.

Her imagination was taking off into the fantasy of her somehow being able to get her hands on some red ink or tomato ketchup for a tremendous nose bleed that would sap her of all energy, when she fell asleep.

It was a couple of hours later that some soft sound nearby had her eyelids fluttering open. Oddly then, maybe because she was sleepily relaxed, when it registered that not only was Chase back, but that he was bending over her, Ashlie felt none of the panic which had seen her so strung up before. Though later it was to dawn on her that the probable reason she did not feel fear was because newly awakened, with Chase looking down at her gently and not at all as aggressive as he had been, she had not then got it all together.

But indeed, she was so unperturbed by him, that vaguely realising the sound that had awakened her must have been the sound of him returning, she had made no attempt to bolt, and the words, 'Did you have a nice walk?' were leaving her in the most natural fashion.

'Beautiful,' replied Chase softly, but his eyes were looking at nowhere but her face.

Her heart rate starting to pick up as his face came a little closer, Ashlie knew a brief confusion that Chase might be saying that it was she who was beautiful and that he had no mind to the beautiful scenery outside. Then, gently, his mouth was over hers.

And all at once, she found herself mesmerised. For she lay there basking in the wonder of such a gentle kiss from the sort of man she knew him to be. But confusion came again, and lingered, when, regardless of whether Chase had been saluting the beauty he thought she had, or had not, she discovered she wanted to know that gentle kiss again.

When she looked up into smiling grey eyes, there was nothing she could do about the invitation in the smile that came to her mouth. And pleasure was hers when, at one with her, a slow gentle smile broke on his mouth too, and softly, tenderly, he kissed her again.

Again it was Chase who pulled back. But it was only when the awareness that she wanted him to kiss her again and to go on kissing her, arrived to rock her, that Ashlie snapped out of the strange twilight world she had found herself in.

'Good grief!' she exclaimed, bringing her left wrist in front of her face as if checking her watch when she had more important things to be doing than to read the dial, 'Is that the time?' She was off the bed like a shot then, and picking up her case *en route*, 'I'd better go and get changed for dinner.' Already she was diving for the bathroom.

Ashlie spent a good half-an-hour in the bathroom. But that was still not sufficient time for her to understand how it was that just the merest touch of Chase Marriner's lips on hers, should have her forgetful of everything but him.

How many more stern lectures was she going to have to give herself before this trauma was through she wondered. Though determined that Chase had kissed her for the last time, Ashlie, knowing that she had to come from the bathroom some time, took a few more moments to steady herself, and then opened the door.

Not lingering in the bedroom, she deposited her case and went through into the sitting room, where she found Chase sitting glancing through a newspaper he must have picked up while he was out.

'The bathroom's all yours,' she advised him when, dropping the newspaper down on the table before him, he stood up.

Why just the fact of him looking at her should make her heart act the giddy-goat, Ashlie had no idea. But she stood motionless as Chase surveyed her in her calf length red crêpe dress with its fine lace collar.

'As I said,' he murmured, taking a pace nearer, 'beautiful.'

'Thank you,' she replied chokily, and drew a relieved breath when he continued walking and went past her into the bedroom.

Her face bereft of make-up since her powder and lipstick were in the handbag she had left in the sitting room, Ashlie retrieved her bag, and with her back to the bedroom, she opted to apply her make-up where she was rather than at the dressing table since Chase could be in any state of undress in the bedroom.

But her application of make-up took only minutes. She took up the paper he had put down, but found that she was too fidgety to be able to read. Again she sought for fresh ideas, the nose bleed along with the sprained ankle having been rejected, but nothing she thought convincing enough inspired her. Just as panic would have taken a hold, she decided, purely for something to do, to turn out her handbag.

Some rest from the disquiet of her thoughts came while sorting through jumble tipped on to the table from her handbag. She wondered why she carried so much around with her, but found when she started to restore each article back to her bag that she had a need for every single item.

That was, until she picked up her passport. That was very definitely superfluous. So too, she thought, taking up the last remaining item, were the francs she had made a special trip to the bank to collect.

'This was supposed to be my treat,' said a good-humoured voice at the back of her.

Jerking round, her throat dried. Speech was taken from her to see that Chase had looked in on her while in the middle of dressing and that, though trouser clad, he had not yet got around to covering his broad manly chest. But when, too sharp not to know the currency in her hand was sufficient enough to be her 'flit from him in Paris' money, he suddenly grinned, try as she might, Ashlie could not stop herself from grinning back.

Sharing this moment of humour with him, she had still not cancelled her grin when all at once as Chase looked at her upward curving mouth, abruptly, his grin had gone.

Her grin swiftly fading, she suddenly felt the very air between them become tense. That tension held her as tightly as it seemed to grip Chase, and as Ashlie felt compelled to keep her eyes on his, so Chase appeared to be unable to take his eyes away from her.

Her very breath choking her, she stared, transfixed, at his face, no sign of humour there now. Then, as if in slow motion, as if without his conscious volition, his hands moved at his sides.

That movement had the spell she was under, broken. And having gained body release, she turned in her chair needing urgently to shut him from her vision. But, unable then to see him, tension was still in her, still in the air. She could feel it—almost touch it.

Chase had not said another word, yet without having heard him move, she knew he had come to stand close to her chair.

Aware of him as never before, Ashlie sat rigid when a hand came to either side of her from behind. Then, those hands were on her arms, not merely touching, but holding her, gripping her. A moment later, she felt a whisper of a kiss to her nape and, as unresisting she sat, in the next instant the pressure had gone from her arms, and she knew she had the room to herself.

Not able to move, Ashlie heard sounds of Chase moving about. And in no time at all, too soon at any rate for her to have recovered from a moment of shared humour changing too swiftly for her to know what it was all about, a fully dressed Chase was back with her.

'Ready?' he enquired, his manner so different, so easy, that she wondered had she imagined that he had been as tense as she! Had she, on edge it seemed ever since she had known him, imagined the whole of it?

Overwhelmingly aware of him, as they walked side by side along the corridor then descended in the lift, Ashlie hoped that her imagination would stay in check and not have her thinking that the owner of every pair of eyes she came into contact with, would know, as the hotel staff did, that they were sharing the same suite, while unmarried.

Wishing that Chase was the type of person who was easily overlooked, instead of having a build and appearance which would always have heads turned to follow his progress, Ashlie stepped out of the lift hearing his suggestion penetrating her thoughts.

'Would you care for a drink before dinner?'

Right at that moment a drink, before dinner or otherwise, seemed to her the best suggestion she'd heard in a long while.

'I'd love one,' she replied. And with his hand at her elbow guiding her in the direction of the lounge bar, she went forwards.

But she was to find that any hopes she might have nursed that a drop of something alcoholic might settle her nerves, were doomed before she had so much as set one foot inside the lounge bar. For when Chase pushed the door open and stood back to allow her to go in front, so as she glanced into the room, Ashlie, as though turned to stone, stopped dead.

Rooted, alarm screaming through her so that even her scalp prickled, her worried eyes saw none of the other people in the room . . . only the two people she had believed to be holidaying somewhere on the Welsh coast!

Shaken to her very soul, she was oblivious of Chase waiting for her to go forward. Appalled, that of all places they should be here—that they had chosen the self-same spot which Chase had chosen for their illicit weekend—all colour left her face. And it was too late then for her to obey the instinct that was insisting that she run away and hide, for as the eyes of the two people she was staring at were drawn to the door, so Ashlie realised—that her parents had seen her!

CHAPTER SIX

SHE stood petrified. Even the hand Chase placed on her arm to propel her forward, which must have been seen by the two people whose eyes were now glued to the door, had no effect in moving her. They must have realised by that, that she was not alone.

But if her mind had been blanked off by her horror, when Chase moved her to one side to allow some people behind access to the room, one glance at her white, stricken face and extreme agitation, was all he needed to know that something was troubling her mightily.

'What is it?' he asked sharply, unknowingly, his frame at her front shielding her from her parents' view.

'My mother and father,' Ashlie whispered desperately, searching in her stunned brain to find a way out of the situation. 'M-my parents—they're *here*!'

That Chase accepted what she told him without any of the panic she was displaying, had Ashlie knowing that it did not matter a damn to him who knew how he chose to spend his weekends. But that he remained cool, as he enquired, 'Your parents, they're not—broad minded?' was to succeed in soothing her agitation a fraction.

'Not where I'm concerned, they're not,' she told him hoarsely.

'Have they spotted us?' Ashlie nodded. But any modicum of agitation she had lost, was to come jetting back when, coolly enough to make her feel like dying where she stood, Chase commented,

'Then, my dear Ashlie, I think you had better introduce me.'

She had no time then in which to recover from his astonishing statement. Even as she started to vigorously shake her head, he had taken the initiative and had left her with no choice but to introduce him, when he moved the shield of his body from in front of her, and Ashlie was again in view of her parents who were now watching the door.

'Look happy,' instructed Chase. She had never felt more unhappy in her life.

But somehow she managed to obey when, with his hand on her arm he forced her forward. Then her eyes took in that there were other people in the room, and that Chase was guiding her away from where her parents were sitting. She shook herself, aware that he could not be expected to know which two she was claiming as her kin—though the surprise both their faces were showing should have given him a hint. She placed her hand on top of the one he had on her arm, and halted him.

'My parents—they're over here.'

Chase smiled, and she knew he had known all along where they were, but that she had without knowing it, acted out a small charade he had instigated to make it look nothing more than natural to anyone watching.

Her father was already on his feet by the time she and Chase reached them. But still in shock, there was no need whatsoever for Ashlie to call on what little acting ability she had, as the exclamation left her:

'What are you doing here?'

'I was just about to ask you the same thing,' replied Hartley Holman, his glance going to Chase and back again to his daughter.

Ashlie delayed a moment too long in replying, but

Chase, giving her a friendly glance, had stepped in to extend his right hand to her father—her father being the nearer to him—and commented, 'Ashlie is so overcome in her pleasure at bumping into you like this, she has forgotten me. Chase Marriner,' he said. And having shaken hands with her father, he moved round the table to shake hands with her mother. And before Ashlie knew it, all four of them were seated round the small table, and her mother, having heard of Chase Marriner from Lynette, and apparently thrilled to bits to meet him—obviously never having heard of his reputation—was smiling:

'My daughter-in-law, Lynette, works in your organisation.' And still smiling prettily, 'Is that how you came to meet Ashlie?'

'Ashlie and I did meet through Lynette,' Chase agreed pleasantly. Ashlie's nerves were electric. She wouldn't put it past him to be shameless enough to tell her mother the exact circumstances of their first meeting. But instead he was taking her mother's thoughts entirely away from how they had met the first time, by telling her, 'Your daughter-in-law, is mostly high thought of.'

Suspecting mockery, Ashlie momentarily lost her nerves as anger flared at the thought that he was sending her mother up. But, shooting him a quick look, her flare of anger died. For the mockery which she knew well enough to spot had he indeed been amusing himself at her mother's expense, was not there.

Having satisfied herself on that point, when her father too joined in the conversation and told Chase how proud they were of their son's wife when they had heard of her promotion, Ashlie began to pin all her hopes on the thought that her parents in their retirement, had decided to pay a return visit to the guest house where they had spent many a happy holiday. And that maybe they had just popped into this particular hotel for a quick aperitif on their way. But her hopes were dashed, and despair set in, when, having lost part of the conversation, she tuned in again and heard her mother say,

'So Hartley said I deserved a little luxury, and didn't tell me that he'd booked us in here for a whole week until we pulled up outside.'

'You're staying here?' she asked faintly.

'I was surprised too,' replied Joan Holman with a light laugh. 'When I saw that this was the way we were heading, I was certain we would be spending the night under Mrs Kemp's roof—you remember Mrs Kemp?' she broke off to ask. But resumed at Ashlie's nod of confirmation that indeed she did remember the pleasant guest-house owner, 'But when we stopped here and your father took the cases out of the car . . .'

Her flow was interrupted when a dinner-jacketed member of staff chose that moment to hover with a set of leather-bound menus. Ashlie was sure she was becoming a candidate for heart failure when she heard Chase's smooth voice as her mother took hold of a menu that was being proffered.

'I'm sure Ashlie would like to spend some time with you. Shall I make it a table for four?'

How, when she was inwardly quaking, she managed to keep a smile on her face, Ashlie did not know. Already the waiter had gone away to arrange a table for four, and she knew that there just wasn't the remotest possibility of her parents not being aware before any meal they shared was at an end, that she and Chase too, were staying at the same hotel.

She had a brief opportunity while her father was

busy coping with her mother's giggles at his French pronunciation as they studied the menu, to hiss, 'Did you *have* to suggest we eat together?' But Chase murmured back, his eyes going to her parents and the evidence there before him that they were every bit as happily married as she had said.

'I can tell them we've changed our minds and would prefer to dine alone in our suite if you like.'

He did not say anything of the sort much to Ashlie's relief, but conversed easily until the time came for the four of them to move from the lounge bar into the restaurant. But her panic soared a moment later, though this time, her father was the cause.

She supposed she had known all along that it would not be long before, believing he had observed all the courtesies, he would politely enquire more into what the daughter whom he had thought in London, was doing so far away from her home. Ashlie had just been served the iced melon she had ordered, about all she thought she could manage. In fear and trembling that the waiter would address her as Mrs Smith or whatever other name Chase had booked her in as, her nerve ends frayed again when her father spoke looking directly to her escort, and not her.

'We had no idea that Ashlie was planning a visit to this area this weekend.'

A spoonful of melon on the way to her mouth, Ashlie lowered her spoon, knowing that inside two minutes, even if Chase did not say outright what this weekend was all about, that for sure, her father being nobody's fool, he would be frowning heavily and have his appetite for his meal taken from him too.

But as her mind went searching for some way to soften the blow of what her father would soon know, Chase was replying. 'Ashlie had no idea either, when we set off. But when I learned of the happy holidays she'd spent in this part of the world and how she loves the Dales, it seemed a small detour for us to make on our way to pay my mother a surprise visit.'

Her father's smile, her mother's smile too, as Joan Holman asked Chase where his mother lived, and the conversation went on from there, were about the only things to reach Ashlie.

Visit his mother! she thought shaken. But whatever tale he was telling her parents about his mother being something of an insomniac and never going to bed before the early hours, Ashlie was too staggered at the realisation that, when she knew full well he would not care a damn what anybody, her parents included, thought of him, his only reason for not telling them about that suite waiting for them upstairs, had to be—because he was protecting her!

'When Ashlie's tummy started to rumble,' Chase was in the middle of quipping when, still shaken, she began again to comprehend the conversation, 'I decided we'd stop here and ring to let my mother know we were on our way, but not to expect us for a meal.'

Both her parents' beamed approval of Chase's decision to stop since it meant that they had a chance to see their daughter, was plain. And her father, in particular, appeared more relaxed now that he knew Mrs Marriner would be chaperoning her that night. Though it was her mother who thought to ask the obvious question.

'Your mother wasn't upset that you and Ashlie will be dropping in on her quite late expecting a couple of beds?'

'My mother loves surprises,' Chase declared, 'and it's quite some time since I last saw her.'

He had no need to say any more. As Ashlie was her father's prized chick, Norris was Joan Holman's first born and although she was always desperately fair, he was that little bit extra special to her. She knew all about the way a lot of mothers saw less of their sons than they would like. And Ashlie knew that if in the days before his marriage, Norris had descended on his old home with a girl in tow, even in the early hours of the morning, then her mother would have been out of her bed like a shot and tearing around making up beds the warmer to welcome them.

'*My* son is in Brazil at the moment,' Joan Holman told Chase a shade wistfully.

Nothing more was required but for Chase to say, 'So Ashlie told me—he's well, I trust?' for her mother to open up at length about Norris, and all he had achieved.

Ashlie ploughed through the rest of her meal, with little to say. Not that she could have said any one word in disagreement with what Chase had told her parents. Besides which, he had skilfully got her mother talking about how proud they were of Norris, and she had no intention of inviting a second inquest. But, she was vastly aware, that even supposing she and Chase made it up to the suite that night without her parents being aware that they were staying in the same hotel—and she had too much to contend with down here to allow herself more panic on what was going to happen once she and Chase did reach that suite—then they risked every chance of again bumping smack bang into them at breakfast!

'You're very quiet, dear.' She looked up to see that her mother had decided that if she wasn't going to bore Chase out of his skull with her talk of Norris and his brilliance—though there was no sign of boredom in him that Ashlie could see—then she had better change the conversation.

'I'm still getting over the shock of seeing you here when I imagined you sunning yourself on the snow-covered beaches of the Welsh coast,' smiled Ashlie, and was relieved to be let off having to say more when her mother turned to Chase to explain for her the remark.

Though when a general move was made to have coffee in the lounge, Ashlie was to discover when she and her mother went in front, that her parent had put her own interpretation for her quiet mood. 'Don't be nervous about meeting Chase's mother, love,' she said quietly, giving her arm a squeeze. 'I'm sure she'll love you.'

She was saved from making any sort of a reply when Chase came forward and opened the lounge door for them. No sooner were they seated though than it became plain to Ashlie that he thought she should by now be over whatever shock she had been in, for he glanced to his watch and asked to be excused.

'I have a business call to put through about now,' he explained. 'Though it shouldn't take long. Meantime,' he smiled, 'I'll leave Ashlie to chat with you.'

Suddenly hating his arrogant confidence that having smoothly soothed any fears her parents might have nursed about the two of them, he could calmly walk away and leave her to deal with a whole bombardment of questions she felt would be coming her way, Ashlie was certain that his excuse of a business call was pure invention.

But she did not have chance to more than wonder why it should bother her that for all he cared, she could well slip up and reveal that the situation was very far from what it seemed, and that it wouldn't

matter a twopenny damn to him, for no sooner had he
gone than her mother was saying with admiration, 'He
must work terribly hard, Ashlie.'

'He—does,' she replied, refraining from adding a
side-swiping, at *play*, as well as at work.

'Are—er—things, serious between you and him?'
her mother went on to ask. Ashlie did not know how
to reply, though to her mind, her efforts to avoid
sharing the same bed as him were mighty serious. But
she was to be grateful for the small respite offered,
when her father chose to interrupt her mother.

'Now, now, Joanie. I know you're longing for the
day Ashlie wears her dress of white, but . . .'

'Well, Chase *is* taking her to introduce her to his
mother,' she replied, as though that meant that the
banns would be read at any minute now. Both parents
then turned to look questioningly at her.

Starting to break out in a cold sweat, but forced to
say something, Ashlie began, 'I'm . . .' Then changed
it to, 'It's—a little early to know yet—how things are
going to turn out.'

She found she was then wishing that Chase would
come back. He was far better at this sort of thing than
she was. She needed him there to fend off her parents'
questions. Hope was still hers, even if she saw it
getting less and less likely by the second, that these
two lovely people would remain in blissful ignorance.

But Chase appeared in no hurry to come back.
Though to her relief Ashlie discovered that her
mother had more control of her curiosity than she had
thought in the circumstances. For except for sending a
fond look to her husband and saying, 'I remember
how secretive I was about my love for you until I
knew that you loved me back,' she had nothing more
to add, but, 'Chase is certainly a gentleman.'

Ashlie smiled to cover her secret hope that the good manners her mother had seen in him, would hold up when, in that suite upstairs, Chase received 'No' for an answer.

But knowing that if she dwelt on such thoughts that her parents, who knew her better than anyone, might glean that she was panicking about something, it was by sheer luck when searching for another subject, that Ashlie thought to steer conversation away from Chase.

'How was Aunt Lilian when you saw her?'

From then on, her Aunt Lilian, having been x-rayed in every conceivable position apparently, was the chief topic of conversation. The diverticulitis which had finally been diagnosed was still under discussion in that where once nobody had ever heard of it, everyone one spoke with these days knew someone else who suffered with it, when, Ashlie unable to keep her eyes from going to the door from time to time, saw it open. This time, it was Chase who came in.

Though why he had been up to their suite and had brought down her car coat—which if her memory hadn't been sunk with the load of all she had got on her mind, she had last seen there—she simply couldn't fathom.

Joan Holman broke off what she was saying when she saw that she had lost her daughter's attention. But a smile came to her, no wonder in her that Ashlie should have more interest in the tall good looking man who was coming over to them, than she should have about her Aunt's insides.

'I think we'd better get on, if you don't mind,' said Chase as he reached them. 'I've just taken a look outside, and it's snowing hard.'

Struck dumb as she grappled with trying to make out what Chase was up to now, Ashlie looked on while he told her father which route he intended to take. But when she had so far not budged an inch, she needed no bigger hint to get to her feet, whatever he was up to, when Chase held out her coat for her to put her arms in.

'You left this in the car. You'l freeze without it once that cold air hits you.'

Her mind was in a whirl. The only thing that impinged upon it was that, from the look of things, she was not going to have to spend another moment fretting about still being in the same hotel as her parents come breakfast time tomorrow.

Then her mother was giving her a tight hug and was saying in an undertone that she must not worry, and repeating that she was sure Mrs Marriner was going to love her, then as she went to shake hands with Chase, Ashlie's father was giving his daughter that same hug.

In less than no time, Ashlie found that she was sitting with Chase in his car, with a veritable snow blizzard raging as the car moved off. With her head still spinning at this sudden turn of events, she tried to work out what was going on.

'Have we checked out of the hotel?' she asked, the night such that with the windscreen wipers doing their best to beat back the onslaught of snow, she thought she could safely deduce that they hadn't left the hotel purely for a joy ride.

'Our cases are in the boot,' he replied, sounding grim.

But if Chase was sounding grim because he was out of sorts that, when it was such a foul night he had turned his back on the comforts of the centrally heated hotel, then Ashlie did not mind. Warmth was spreading through her that he had used making a business call to cover his absence while he went to pack, not only his own belongings, but hers also. It warmed her through and through that, having seen her on the brink of having kittens ever since she had seen her parents, when for himself he wouldn't give a damn, he had for her sake checked out of the hotel.

All antipathy was to go from her then. That warmth of feeling got the better of her, she forgot entirely that she might well fare better if Chase remained totally fed up with her. She just had to say quietly,

'Thank you, Chase.'

He did not answer. Though with there being no sign of the blizzard they were driving through letting up, to Ashlie it did not matter. And for the next half-an-hour, with the weather conditions dictating their slow speed, she left him to concentrate on his driving.

Chase was turning out to be much more of an enigma than she had thought at the start. She played back in her mind everything that had happened since he had opened that lounge bar door, maybe because of the convincing way he had told her parents that they were on their way to see his mother, quite off the top of her head, she was moved to ask,

'Are we really going to your mother's home?'

For her sins, she was promptly shot down in flames. Chase did not so much as take his eyes from the road, and for that Ashlie was grateful. Without knowing why, she was hurt enough for tears to sting her eyes when whipping back, came his aggressive retort,

'I've never taken any woman home to *"meet Mother"* yet—I'm not about to start.'

Put very firmly in her place, Ashlie was all at once feeling too dispirited to retaliate with the jibe that if his mother was anything like him, then she considered he was doing her a favour.

The lights of a building up in front came nearer and

nearer, and he pulled the car off the road, to cut the engine at a small hotel. She knew then, as he went and opened up the boot, that from somewhere she was going to have to rally every scrap of spirit.

That Chase looked as grim as he sounded when, with one case under his arm, and one in his hand, he helped her with his free hand across the snow and into the hotel, was not instrumental in making her returning fears abate.

He was not looking well pleased she could see, that there was no one on duty at the reception desk. His apparent annoyance grew when he had to wait for someone to come and tell him that, though many travellers had pulled in off the road, they thought they could accommodate them.

Again Ashlie left it to him to fill in the registration documents, panic again trying to take a hold when she saw that with Chase looking as impatient as the devil, he wouldn't be in any mood to put up with her prevarications when the crunch came and he—having turned amorous—told her the moment of reckoning was here.

Her legs had started to feel decidedly wobbly, when his hand came to her arm, and, with his voice terse he directed, 'This way.' Adding curtly, 'If this "hotel" does boast the services of a porter, I'm not inclined to wait for him to show himself.'

From that she saw that, in impatience to get to their room, Chase had sorted out for himself which way they were to go.

Feeling drained of energy, she followed where he led. And when after a flight of stairs and a walk along a corridor, Chase stopped at one of the doors and inserted a key in the lock, she felt defeated before the battle had even begun.

But, enigma just did not begin to describe the man who was pushing her inside the room. For while she was doing her best to keep her eyes away from the bed—no suite for them this time—Chase had placed her case down, and had straightened to look down at her defeated expression. Then, while she was preparing to fight him, he made her stare dumbfounded when, coldly, he told her, 'My room's down the hall—I'll see you in the morning.'

'You'll—see me in the m-morning?' she choked, uncomprehending, her eyes big in her face, that when they both knew what this weekend was about, Chase, had, by the sound of it, booked them into separate rooms!

Though she was not to have to wait long to be enlightened, and there was no doubting, with his next gritty comment, that Chase Marriner was completely and utterly fed up with her and the whole business.

'I like my women willing—and not looking as if they're going to burst into tears at any moment.'

He might have gone then without saying another word. But, as the penny dropped that not only did he not want an unwilling woman in his bed—and that quite clearly he was too fed up to want to bother himself to do anything to change her to be ardently willing—and that she was to have that bed to herself, something broke in Ashlie.

'Oh, Chase,' she said in her relief. And the next second, without the smallest conscious thought, she had gone forward to him.

What she did want from him she had no idea for the moment. But that Chase forgot his ill temper for a brief while and, dropping his case to the floor, stretched out his arms to take hold of her, was to give her such a degree of comfort, than only then was she to know what it was she did want from him.

And that knowledge hers, she did not want to move from him. Held like that against his heart, she never wanted this moment to end.

But it was for only seconds that she was to know where home was—with him. For, without so much as attempting to kiss her, Chase was then abruptly pushing her away.

'Get some rest,' he ordered shortly, and in one movement, he had picked up his case, and was gone.

Ashlie lay awake for a long time that night. It would have been impossible for her to go to sleep anyway while her eyes refused to remain dry. And even without her tears, she had more than enough on her mind to keep her sleepless.

Why him? cried her heart. Why Chase? Why, she had to ask, the reason for her feeling of euphoria at lunchtime now known to her—the reason there why Chase had been able to do what he had to her senses before then; from almost the first moment of meeting him—why had she to go and fall in love with *him*?

Why had she to give her heart to a man who, uncaring, could so easily drop one woman for another, and who would never stay faithful to any one woman. To a man, a philanderer, who had shown that for tonight—tomorrow being another day—that even a brief affair with her had no appeal. An unfathomable man who, without his endorsement of 'I've never taken any woman home to "*meet Mother*" yet—I'm not about to start' she had known in advance, even if he did care for her—which he did not; even if he was marriage minded—which he was not; was a man who was just not marriage material.

CHAPTER SEVEN

ASHLIE had nursed a hope that her feelings for Chase were nothing more than a fleeting tenderness for the way, when seeing her next door to tears, he had last night held her to him. But when she answered the door to his knock the following morning, she knew the uselessness of that hope. He seemed in little better humour for his night's sleep, for his first words were sharp.

'Bring your case. We'll get off straight after breakfast.'

'We're leaving!' she exclaimed.

He threw her a hostile look as he moved past her and into her room. 'It was never my idea to have single rooms,' he bit out sharply. His impatience about last night obviously returned when, as though he would do her packing for her if she didn't shift herself, he hefted her case from the luggage stand, and tossed it to the bed.

Any weakness that seeing him had brought, was to swiftly vanish. Mutiny replaced it that, like an idiot, she had credited him with all sorts of kindness which he just did not possess. The only reason he had left her alone last night was because, weary no doubt from driving through that blizzard and a double room clearly not available, he had favoured a comfortable night's sleep rather than have his long length cramped up close to her in a bed that was barely three quarter size.

With her face reflecting the thought that Chase

Marriner was not her favourite person that morning,
Ashlie hurried to throw her few things into her case.
She was of a mind then to tell him that it had never
been in her head that they should share a double. For
two pins she would have told him right then that he
could forget any notion he had of booking out of this
hotel and into one that did have accommodation
available which was more to his liking.

She had barely snapped her case closed before he
had taken it from the bed and was striding to the door.
Her mutinous rage was fanned higher when she almost
had to trot to keep up with him as they went along the
corridor, and down the flight of stairs. Her mutiny
soared so that she wanted to hit him, when in the
small foyer, he grunted, 'Wait here,' and strode off to
take their cases out to his car.

To think, she fumed, that she had lain awake most
of the night crying over him! My God, she needed her
head looking at!

Within the two minutes of waiting for him to come
back, and another minute spent in watching the snow
framed glass door for sight of him, Ashlie had to admit
that her anger with him was purely and simply a
defence mechanism, and no more. She loved the brute,
and however much he upset her, near him was where
she wanted to be.

Someone coming down the stairs behind made her
aware she was not giving them much room to get by.
She had just moved a few steps nearer to the door
when Chase appeared and put his hand to the handle.
Her mutiny gone, Ashlie struggled with the fear that
she might be weak enough to smile at him, which
could cause him to wonder at the change in her. Not
trusting herself, she swiftly turned her back as Chase
came in.

An automatic apology came to her lips that her swift action had caused her to bump into the person about to pass behind her. But that apology was never to be heard. For where her eyes were blind to anything except that it was some male she had bumped into, a masculine voice was exclaiming,

'Ashlie—darling!'

Shaken to hear her name, let alone the 'darling' that went with it, her head shot up. 'Kevan Salter!' she said surprised. But she had no need to wonder why, when once she had thought him the bees knees, he should now leave her cold. She had once thought herself in love with the man who was giving her the benefit of his cheesey grin as though wanting to impress her that he still had every one of his thirty-two teeth, but that had been before she had so painfully discovered exactly how it felt to be 'in love'.

'You're as beautiful as ever, I see.' He brought his brand of charm into play. 'But what are you . . .' That was as far as he got before Chase came and planted himself firmly at her side.

Glancing at his thunderous expression, Ashlie guessed he was none too pleased that this appeared to be the weekend in her life that had been set aside for her to bump into people she knew. Though, aware that she had been remiss with her introductions last night, she ignored his expression.

'Chase, this is Kevan Salter. Kevan . . .'

'You'll excuse us,' grunted Chase, cutting through her attempt at poise. This morning he was evidently not in favour of being introduced, 'My fiancée and I want to be away as soon as possible.'

Ashlie did not then have so much as a moment in which to blink at Chase claiming her as his fiancée. His right arm was about her shoulders, and whether the breakfast room was where she wanted to go, or whether it wasn't, the pressure of that arm at the back of her was ensuring that that was where she was going.

His arm fell away when he selected a table and pulled out a chair for her. But, as it flitted through her mind to wonder what the blazes she had ever seen in Kevan, mutiny was back with her that Chase could be so overbearingly high-handed and rude.

Though if he had observed her unsmiling expression, he was in no mood to be placatory. For, barely had he sat down himself, than he was snarling accusations at her.

'Is there nowhere you can go where you're not known by somebody?'

'Apparently not,' she answered snappily.

'Who was he?' Chase fired then. Ashlie batted away as ridiculous the notion that Chase sounded like some jealous lover, of which he was neither, jealous or lover, and turned to the waitress who was at their table to take their order.

By the time she had gone, Ashlie had lost all inclination to fire back that if Chase had not been so downright rude and had waited until she had completed the introduction, then he might have heard, without needing to ask, who Kevan was.

'Well?'

'Kevan is someone I used to work for,' she answered sourly, her ire rising that when Chase asked a question, he demanded an answer.

'Good God!' he then exclaimed. 'Is *he* the one you're in love with?'

From that, she could only guess, that having seen Kevan once, and no doubt having sized him up straight away, Chase did not think much to him.

'I never said I was still in love with him,' she snapped.

'But you are?'

'Did you have to claim me as your fiancée?' Ashlie countered, fed up with his dog-with-a-bone insistence, and hoping to get him off the subject of Kevan.

'Want Salter to know you're still free?'

Ashlie knew then that Chase was just spoiling for a fight. She looked away, all of a sudden not wanting to fight with him.

Other people had come down to breakfast, she saw. Intent on not looking at Chase her glance moved on to where Kevan sat. He had the same practised look of adoration on his face for his blonde companion, which had fooled her all those months ago into believing that he wanted to marry her. That Kevan had brought the blonde to this out-of-the-way place for the sort of weekend he had once proposed that she should spend with him, was plain to Ashlie. And although that in itself had little effect on her save for her to be grateful for her lucky escape, what did affect her, and make her feel sick in her stomach, was that any of the other guests waiting for breakfast, could be looking at her and Chase and thinking the same about them—and be right. She *was* there with him for an illicit weekend, and even if Chase had seen before her how they might look, and for that reason claim her to Kevan as his fiancée, Ashlie just could not take it.

Their order had still not arrived when, unaware that Chase had followed her eyes, she blurted, 'Can we go?'

'What's the matter?' he snarled. 'Can't you take watching him make eyes at his new mistress?'

Ashlie felt the sting of tears that when she wanted to be gone from there, Chase was still aggressively looking for a fight.

She shook her head. 'It—isn't that,' she said chokily.

'What then?' he asked, unconvinced.

She doubted he would understand, but, her voice reduced to a whisper, emotion there in her face, 'It's all so—so sordid,' she said huskily, and had to look down to the tablecloth.

She didn't know for how much longer she was going to be able to sit there. But before she could follow through the impulse to go and wait outside until Chase had eaten his breakfast, suddenly he was on the move.

Without further comment he was on his feet and without fuss, his expression inscrutable, he was pulling back her chair and was guiding her out to the foyer. It was there, his face giving nothing of his thoughts away, that he handed her some keys.

'Wait in the car,' he instructed.

No argument in her, Ashlie left him to pay for their night's lodging, and felt, when spring was only just around the corner, the icy blast of a freezing winter's day when she put her nose outside. An attempt had been made to clear a path to the car park, but apart from that, the whole area lay under a blanket of snow.

That gave her something else on which to pin her thoughts. Whichever direction Chase had decided they go, the road conditions looked to be too treacherous for more than the most careful driving. Thus distracted Ashlie had recovered a little from the sick, feeling of distaste that had taken her in the breakfast room, when Chase joined her.

'I'm sorry you had to miss your breakfast,' she apologised quietly, when, her love and her conscience proved too much for her.

His look, when he delayed setting off, was as arctic as the weather, she observed. And she was to wish she had not bothered to apologise, when he turned on her icily.

'Is this the first time you've been part of the *sordid scene*?'

'You're the first man I've ever been away with,' she replied, and saw that he could still believe, to use his expression, that she had 'been between the sheets' elsewhere other than at an hotel. But from the uncivil look he threw her as he set the car in motion, she knew that whatever she said that day, was not going to please him.

Any sign posts that would have meant anything to her were obliterated by snow, and those that were readable gave her no clue to where they were going. A car driver herself Ashlie knew, as they crawled along in a build up of traffic, that Chase was going to need to keep all his wits about him if he was going to get them anywhere in one piece.

She was silent more because she had nothing she wanted to say to him, than from having any thought that he would need to concentrate of the road. But when with snow again falling heavily, they had seemed to have been on the road for hours, though the car clock telling her that barely an hour-and-a-half had gone by, so Ashlie began again to grow all knotted up inside.

She had guessed, apart from the fact that Chase had limited patience and would not be content to crawl along at this pace for very much longer, that the first respectable looking hotel they came across would see him pulling off the road. But the way things were going this weekend, she wasn't going to take bets that at their next stopping place they wouldn't bump into either his mother, or his father, or even a crowd from where she worked having, unbeknown to her, their annual outing.

Five minutes later, the thought had moved to the idea that they could well meet up with some old flame of his. Ashlie's inner tumult magnified, and turned to anger. She was unconcerned then about whatever foul road conditions they were traversing. And with pugnacity building up that, as agreed, she had been away for the weekend hadn't she? Ashlie broke into his concentration belligerently.

'I want to go home.'

'What the hell do you think I'm trying to do but get back as fast as I can!' came flying snarling back at her before she could draw another breath.

The wind well and truly taken from her sails, she was stumped to make any sort of a reply. Yet she felt contrarily hurt that from his 'as fast as I can' it seemed that Chase couldn't wait to get them back so that he could get rid of her.

Well, that went double for her, she thought, pride rousing her to resentment. She'd be equally pleased to see the last of him too, she railed. But her whipped up aggression departed when Chase switched on the radio to catch the news. She saw his jaw clench at the information that with most of the country in the grip of the same wintry conditions, that there was a threat of all roads freezing over come nightfall, and that the motorway he had obviously been making for, had now been closed.

They had taken the long route to Yorkshire for her benefit. But it was not from any thought for her to see the picturesque countryside that Chase was going to take the long route back. He had no other choice.

Beginning to feel the pangs of hunger, her conscience was again to smite her that, through her, Chase with a bigger frame to fill, had missed his breakfast. Though with traffic slipping and sliding all over the place, she thought he had enough to contend with in keeping his car on the road than to think of food. But then Chase pulled up at the next pub they came to.

The stop, however, was brief, with Chase pointing out the ladies powder room, while he went and arranged some sandwiches for them to eat as they went. Minutes later they were back on the road, with no let up in the appalling weather conditions.

They had been forced to go at a wearisome snail's pace for an age when Ashlie volunteered, 'Shall I drive for a while?'

'No,' was her short sharp answer. She did not ask again.

Darkness had descended before they reached striking distance of Hertfordshire. But though, as they had been warned, it had started to freeze, she was glad to see that there was not so much snow about the further south they came.

Her home was on the other side of London, but it made obvious sense to her that Chase should take the road that would take them straight to Clarendon House. Apart from the fact that his home was the nearer, and that he must want to get from behind the wheel as soon as he could, she had her car to pick up.

It was some time after nine when they pulled up at Clarendon House, and her car, now snow covered, was exactly where she had left it. Ashlie got out of Chase's car and, aware that as well as being fed up that he was doubtless tired and irritable, she sought for tact to say what had to be said before she took off.

But to knock her out of her stride, Chase was already up the steps and turning his key in the lock, and, clearly expecting her to follow, he was holding the door open for her to go through. Left with no alternative but to go after him, it was not tact but something less sweet that came to her tongue with the thought that once again he was being high-handed.

To keep out the cold air, she closed the front door behind her, then trailed after him into the drawing room where Chase was stirring a welcoming fire in the hearth to flame.

'Before I leave,' she addressed his back while he placed a couple of logs on the flames, 'there's something . . .'

'Leave!' he said harshly, straightening as he turned to show her a no-nonsense expression. 'You're not going *anywhere.*'

Astonished, she just gaped. He had to be tired out from that hours and hours long wearisome drive, but, by the sound of it, he still had energy enough, and was not so fed up with her, that he could still mean to make love to her. Ashlie putting him right about that without more than a second's delay.

'Our agreement has been fulfilled,' she told stonily. 'I've been away with you as I said I would. It wasn't my fault that . . .'

'Stow it,' he cut in grimly. Adding over his shoulder as he strode past her and out through the door, 'You're not driving anywhere in these conditions.'

Left staring vacantly at the empty doorway, Ashlie was too stunned to move. When Chase had refused her offer to take the wheel on the way down, she had thought it because he had an aversion to trusting his plush car to a mere female. But, motionless where she stood, her heart picking up a hurried beat, she understood that with the roads icing over, he was not in favour of her driving her own car either.

For all of one minute, Ashlie was in a fantasy world where Chase would not allow her to drive because he was afraid that some harm might befall her. But unpleasant common sense soon arrived to hit that foolish notion on the head. Which left her back with the only reason Chase Marriner insisted she would drive herself nowhere that night, was because he had other plans for her.

Anger stormed in then, and had her marching from the drawing room. But only for her to meet Chase when he came through the front door with their cases.

If he observed her angry mutinous expression, he did not comment on it, but said, 'Since I didn't know what time we'd arrive, or if we'd arrive at all tonight, I told Mrs Parry we'd forage for ourselves.'

'*You* forage for *yourself*,' Ashlie snapped heatedly, as it penetrated that he must have phoned his housekeeper from the pub they had stopped at. But that he was unmoved that she had no desire to 'forage' with him, and showed not the slightest inclination to hand over her case, had her thinking that she could manage very well without it, thank you.

In the next moment she was out through the front door rejoicing in the opinion that since Chase had made no move to stop her, he knew when he was licked. She was still fuming when having scraped the snow from the windscreen of her car, she inserted her key into the ignition.

That her car would not start was about all she needed. No way could she coax it into life. Exasperation had her glaring at the illuminated front door of the house. She knew though, that it was useless to expect that door to open and for Chase to come out to see if he could help to get her going.

She stared in frustration at the car bonnet for some minutes, aware that with her lack of mechanical knowledge that to scrape the snow from off the lid and take a look inside for the trouble would be a complete waste of time. Then it suddenly clicked. There was no snow on the bonnet! The bonnet had recently been lifted and that—somebody—had already taken a look inside! She was back to blasting Chase with a vengeance.

The swine! The diabolical swine! The cunning ... Fury like none she had ever known had her charging back to the house, slamming the front door behind her to herald her arrival.

She found Chase in the kitchen emptying a can of soup into a saucepan. Though before she could get a word in, he spoke, without so much as a glance her way, entirely unconcerned with the guilt he should be showing.

'I'll restore the rotor arm in the morning.' His tone was cool.

'If you think for a moment that I'm going to sleep with you tonight,' spat Ashlie furiously, spurred on that he was making no attempt to deny he had disabled her car but had openly admitted it, 'then do *you* have another think coming.'

The soup having been poured into the saucepan with fine precision, Chase spared her a glance. 'Should I care to take you,' he coldly replied, 'I would soon have you willing, and you know it. But,' he went on stingingly, ignoring that she looked ready to explode, 'since my time with you has been a disaster from start to finish,' you'll forgive me for wondering what pleasure I ever thought we might share this weekend in the first place.'

She felt as though he had just slapped her. All anger in her was nullified. She had been as good as told that he would as soon cuddle up to a porcupine. Tears came to her eyes, causing her to be glad his attention was on the saucepan he was placing on the stove.

But, as pride reared in her to push those tears back, one thing had been settled. With her car immobile— his only idea in removing that rotor arm to save himself the chore of turning out to pull her from some ditch if she went off the road anywhere near Clarendon House—then from what he had just said, Chase had gone completely off the idea of having her in his bed. Indeed now he would probably turf her *out*, in the unlikely event of her climbing in with him.

She had wept copious tears over him last night, but the tears of hurt she was crying inside, had to be bottled down. And as she watched him take hold of a loaf of bread, she did not want to go near him, or to do a thing to help. But when first one misshapen chunk of bread was sliced and he had the knife half-way down another ragged uneven wodge, it was more than she could do to stand idly by and watch the ham-fisted way he was going about it.

'Get out of the way,' she said belligerently, 'and give me that bread knife.' Loftily he looked up, but she wasn't in any mood to be polite. 'Go and stir the soup,' she ordered, 'and don't let it boil.'

That, without argument, he gave up the bread knife and went to stir the soup had her knowing that, having said his piece, he saw no point in trivial argument.

Soup, scrambled eggs on toast, and cheese and biscuits were eaten in the kitchen. And by the time Ashlie was sipping coffee, she had resolved that, before she cleared up the kitchen and went to bed, there was one other matter which had to be cleared up too. She'd had to accept that she would be going to her office straight from Clarendon House tomorrow, and since that meant making an early start, what had to be established could not be left until the morning.

'Am I to have the same room I had on Friday?' she

asked, when she thought she had got it all sorted out in her head.

'Mrs Parry will have re-made your bed,' he confirmed, to remind Ashlie of how she had stripped the bed on Saturday morning. It was obvious that he had decided hours ago that she would not be driving that night. It was all part of the forward planning that was, she supposed, second nature to him.

'When I leave in the morning, do I leave with your word that. . .' she faltered, but made herself go on, '. . . that you won't pay my sister-in-law any more attention than her work for you demands?'

From the glowering look that came to his face, she guessed he must be wondering why the hell he should give up Lynette when having deprived himself of her company for the weekend in favour of an alternative, that alternative weekend had turned out to be such a farce.

She braced herself for the full-scale row that would surely come the moment Chase uttered the words 'Like hell' or whichever way he chose to express it. But Ashlie was to find that there was a fairness in him which he would not go against. For, bluntly though it was put, he churlishly gave her the answer she wanted.

'I suppose—since you would have come across—I owe you that much.'

The time to tell him that 'come across' she would have not, was not now, unless she wanted to invite a few more of his blunt comments. But with the objective she had had from the beginning achieved— Norris's marriage safe, without her having lain with Chase—Ashlie felt none of the joy which only a few days ago such a conclusion would have brought her.

'Thank you,' she said quietly, a heaviness in her heart that 'conclusion' said it all. She was in love with

Chase, but tomorrow when she said goodbye, she would never see him again.

With everything said, she saw there was nothing else to be done but to set the kitchen to rights, and to go up to bed—though what sleep she hoped to get, she didn't know.

Observing that Chase had finished his coffee, she took his cup and saucer with her own over to the sink, and began to run hot water into a bowl. Though when she returned to the table for more of the things they had used, it was only to have him tell her as he looked up,

'Leave the dishes, Mrs Parry will attend to them in the morning.'

Ashlie flicked a glance to his aristocratic head. Weighted down with inner unhappiness as she was, the memory of how he'd consigned himself to patience during the fatiguing hours behind the driving wheel flushed out a tenderness in her.

'You must be worn out,' she said softly, unthinkingly. 'Why don't you go up to bed.' Damning the weakness he wrought in her, Ashlie caught his sharp look, and knew that something guaranteed to offend was on its way—if she didn't beat him to it. 'I'm not leaving this kitchen in this tip for Mrs Parry to find in the morning,' she told him in no uncertain terms, a marked aggressive change in tone there in her voice.

She expected then that she was going to be on the receiving end of an earful of something unpleasant. But suddenly, while she was glaring at him, and Chase was looking back at her stern-faced, she had a definite feeling that his sense of humour was getting the better of him. She could swear from the quirk of movement at the corners of his mouth, that he was about to break into a grin.

Swiftly, her love rising up again, she grabbed at the rest of the crockery and went over to the sink. She had started on the washing up, when she heard his voice, not short, not looking for a fight, meekly ask, 'Am I allowed to help with the drying?'

Her spirits straight away took off on an upward zoom. Her own grin threatened to break loose and she was aware of how only a minute ago, weakness had made her voice soft for him. She gave her answer by a nod of her head, but with the atmosphere all at once lighter, her grin was to push for release from all angles when she saw him pick up a tea towel.

Their combined efforts had the washing up finished in no time. But those few minutes of sharing a chore with Chase in such a contrasting atmosphere from what had been, had her wanting more, for all too soon, he would be out of her life.

Not trusting her voice, unable to say a word lest her voice came out all choked and gave him some idea that those moments of washing dishes, when he had forgotten to be the uncivil brute he had been all that day, were little short of precious to her, she headed out of the kitchen.

To find Chase right there beside her made her hard put to remember where she had left her case. Then she recalled that he had been carrying both the cases when she had dashed past him to go to her car.

With no sign of luggage in the hall, Ashlie glanced in through the open drawing-room door. Both cases she saw, were just inside the room where he had left them to go and 'forage' in the kitchen.

Doing her best to act normally, though by then she was beginning to wonder what normal was—for nothing as far as she could remember had been normal in any way since she had known Chase—Ashlie stepped through the drawing-room doorway.

She spent a moment or two in making sure her voice would behave and not betray the emotion she was feeling. Before she could get out the light 'I'll say goodnight and go to my room' which she had ready though Chase beat her to it.

'I'm about ready to turn in,' he commented. The humour that had pushed its way up through his sour mood was breaking through again, and it was to be her undoing, when, with his mouth taking on an upward curve, he added, 'That is unless you've decided we've got to hoover the whole bloody house before I get to my bed.'

Fractured, the grin she had managed to suppress, would be held in no longer. And, made helpless as her sense of humour rose up and met his, she giggled, her eyes alight with laughter, as a wide grin parted her lips.

All feelings of dejection disappeared from her, a brief happiness was hers, and would not go away even when the matching grin went from Chase, and he just stood and stared at her shining eyes and parted mouth.

At that her grin faded too. Suddenly, as if against his will, Chase said, 'Your face takes on more than beauty when you laugh.' The serious way in which he said it; the stilled look of him the moment before an involuntary sort of movement brought him nearer as if to examine her beauty more closely, made all her laughter die, and another, more intense, emotion take its place.

Her heart drumming, she saw that those grey eyes that looked deeply into hers no longer held the ice that had been in them for most of the day. Only warmth was in those grey eyes now and, as though hypnotised, she could not look away.

Lost to anything and everything, Ashlie felt tension growing in him as it was growing in her, but still she could not look from him.

'Oh God!' she heard him groan beneath his breath. And his hands were coming out for her when she heard the tortured sound, 'What a torment you are to me,' and he moved to take her in his arms.

There was no thought in her to avoid his kiss. She wanted his kiss, she needed his kiss. It was like coming home to feel his mouth over hers. And once begun, Chase as if hungry for her mouth too, did not stop at one kiss.

Ardently he pressed her to him, his hands at her back, moulding her to him. Her heart hammered with the knowledge that despite what Chase had said, he had not stopped wanting her. She felt powerless, just as she had been when his lips had touched hers before. She could not resist him.

Straining to him, wanting, needing this closeness, this touching, this holding, Ashlie had no clear notion when Chase had moved with her until they were nearer to where the log fire glowed and flamed in the hearth. Her senses were enflamed too, she was on fire for him as they sank down to the thick-piled hearth rug. The warmth from the fire caressed her skin the way, her dress now unzipped and falling from her shoulders, his hands were caressing her skin.

'Sweet, sweet Ashlie,' he breathed, and captured her lips.

When he went to trail kisses down her throat, she pulled back her head to luxuriate in the thrill of him, of what he was doing to her and to her senses as his lips sought and plundered the valley between her breasts.

A moment's shyness took her as his hands

whispered over the silky smooth skin of her shoulders and moved down to unhook her bra. She clutched on to him in her shyness, needing a brief moment to let go the inhibitions of her girlhood.

But, shyness overcome, she relaxed her hold on him, her lips going to the side of his face, a message there in that kiss, of her complete surrender, of her complete willingness to go wherever he led.

Pink came to her face when Chase looked down to her swollen bared breast, but only for her to know more rapture when he bent to kiss each pink-pinnacled hardened tip. A sigh of enchantment left her, when his warm hands came to hold her breasts, to cup them, and to fondle.

A fierce flame of desire was burning in his eyes, and Ashlie wanted him. Wanted him and wanted to feel his naked skin too, just as he was touching her. And she knew more delight when, her fingers suddenly all thumbs at the buttons of his shirt, his hands left the mind-spinning caressing of her spine to help her.

'Oh Chase,' she cried, when he guessed at her need and pulled her close until she felt the burning touch of the skin of his chest against her breasts. 'I want you so,' she murmured.

'I want you, little darling,' he answered hoarsely, and again he kissed her, his mouth still over hers as he brought her to lie down on the warm rug, his body coming over hers so that she flew beyond rapture.

When Chase removed her dress entirely, Ashlie knew that, soon, she would be his. And she gloried in the feel of him when, clad only in his briefs, he came again to lie over her.

But again she was made aware that Chase was no opportunist lover. Having aroused her senses to fever pitch, and with the passion in his kisses growing deeper and yet deeper, that fierce flame in his eyes telling her that he wanted her as passionately as she wanted him, it was her comfort he thought of, when softly he breathed,

'Here, by the fire, little love? Or . . .'

'Here,' whispered Ashlie, her need for him swamping her. Only the barrier of lingering shyness preventing her from adding, 'Now, take me now.'

Her shyness was there again when Chase, his caressing fingers at her hips and on her last vestige of clothing, began to ease from her that last piece of covering. And she was then clutching on to him, her fingers digging into his bare upper arms in a jerky spasm of uncontrolled movement. Chase halted, ardour there in his smile, his look gently questioning.

'I'm—sorry,' she whispered, an answering smile there on her face. 'Be patient with me.'

That her words were no sort of answer to why, when he had heard her state that she wanted him, she had clutched at him like that, was evident that his look though still warm on her, had not lost that trace of puzzlement.

'Patient, sweet love?' he asked, that gruff note of wanting in his voice there to thrill her.

Not wanting to talk, but wanting instead that Chase should kiss her again, Ashlie saw that the sooner she explained, the sooner would she feel the warmth of his mouth against her own again.

'I'm a bit . . . shy, I think,' she confessed, feeling then so completely at one with him, that she thought she would be able to tell him anything.

A smile curving his mouth, Chase tenderly queried, 'Shy—at this stage—when I'm about to make you mine?' There seemed to be no reason why she should not confess, her voice husky with her own need.

'I've never made love before. I . . .'

A fleeting moment ago Chase had been as close to her as a second skin, but now, not one part of him was touching her. He was sitting staring at her as though he just could not credit his hearing. That should have been enough to warn her that something was wrong. But, with her need for him still passionate upon her, if there was something not quite right about the way he had sprung away from her, then Ashlie had no hope whatsoever of seeing what it was.

Chase, a peculiar kind of shock seeming to be in him, did not immediately come back to her, but, with a cracked sound there in his voice, he asked, 'What— did you say?'

Ashlie knew that if what she had said had been instrumental in taking him from her, then, wanting him back, she was not going to repeat it.

'Please Chase,' she said, and hoped he would need to hear no more than that to know that sitting where he was, was not where she wanted him to be. But her plea for him to come back to her was ignored. He was insisting that she answered.

'Did I hear you right?' he questioned, his stern expression in total contrast to the desire-filled expression he had worn before. 'Have you just told me,' he pressed, 'that you're a virgin?'

At his persistence, Ashlie came a little way down from the dizzy heights his lovemaking had taken her to. He was forcing her reply. 'Yes,' she answered, 'I've . . .' It was as far as she got.

'Good God!' exploded from him. Shock waves reached her. 'Do you mean to tell me you went away with me—willing to let me take your virginity,' he roared, 'purely to save a marriage that . . .' he broke off, words failing him.

But not so Ashlie. Her descent from that upper, unthinking plane, once started, had accelerated swiftly downwards. And, torn apart inside, and as near as naked before him as made no difference, having been so slow off the mark as to be immobile, she had caught on fast. Quickly she grabbed up her dress and while she struggled into it, she was yelling too.

'I had no intention whatsoever of—of sleeping with you when we went away. I knew you thought I would, but I wouldn't have. I . . .'

But Chase had surmounted the shock of her innocent disclosure, and was furiously chopping her off. 'You've just *proved* that, haven't you! Not two minutes ago I had you mine for the taking,' he snarled. 'There wasn't so much as an iota of resistance about you then, nor would there have been . . .'

'Well there is now!' she shrieked. Her dream world had so abruptly taken on nightmare proportions that she was shaking badly. To be reminded how utterly without resistance he had made her, it was more than she could take then to stand there arguing about it.

With what dignity there was to be found with her dress still unzipped and a bra snatched up in one hand, Ashlie scooped up her case and raced from the room. Tears began the moment she had the bedroom door closed.

CHAPTER EIGHT

WHEN she opened her eyes the next morning, Ashlie was resigned to the fact that Chase Marriner was going to take some ousting from her heart and her head. Thoughts of him had been with her before her eyes had even opened.

She thought it highly unlikely that he would take it into his head to bring her a cup of tea as he had the last time she had spent a night in his home, but it was still early when, washed and dressed she was ready to go to her office.

She shook with agitation as she slipped her nightshirt into her case and snapped the locks. Cringing mortification overcame her as, the memory refusing to leave her alone, she thought of her wild and—as Chase hadn't hesitated to remind her—unresisting response. Oh, if only she could leave Clarendon House without having to see him again.

But she was haunted by the memory of how she had been and, womaniser, rake, philanderer that he was, how he had been. She could not tie up how that something in him had stopped him from taking her virginity—something which no self-respecting philanderer would take account of. Ashlie found she could no longer stay in her room waiting for everyone else to start their day.

But as she hurriedly left her room, she found evidence that she was not the only one astir. She had almost reached the bottom of the stairs when hot colour surged to her face. And that was *before* Chase, on his way in from outside, looked up and saw her.

Pride made her meet his eyes full on. And pride it was that had her head tilting that small degree higher when, after a weak hesitating moment, she continued on her way downstairs.

Chase waited until she was within a few steps of him before he spoke. She had seen that he was in a foul mood, before she saw his mouth tighten at her scarlet colour.

'I'll get Mrs Parry to attend to your breakfast,' he grunted, then paused to add the unsmiling after-thought, 'Can you find your own way to the breakfast room?'

Solemnly she nodded. But when he went striding away in search of his housekeeper, Ashlie had something on her mind other than breakfast.

She watched Chase until he went out of sight then, praying that her surmise was right and that he had just come in from returning the rotor arm to her car, she was haring back up the stairs.

A few minutes later, her case flung on to the back seat, she was in her car and going as fast as she could down the snow covered drive.

Road conditions had improved by the time she was within a mile of her office. But, in a moment of lost concentration having had one near skid Ashlie brought her thoughts back from Chase and how his reaction would be a non-reaction when he found that she, along with her car had gone.

Presuming that Lynette would have gone to work today after all, the thought came during the morning to give her a ring. But she changed her mind. Lynette was invariably up to her eyes at work, and had partly assumed that she wouldn't see her back from her visit to her parents until tonight anyway. And apart from anything else, since Lynette would be feeling as

unhappy as she was feeling, and for the same reason—
Lynette too had been rejected by Chase—she thought
she could well wait until the evening to hear how
Lynette had not gone to Paris after all.

Though there were a lot of sins that Ashlie, in
morose moments, could lay at Chase Marriner's door,
she felt strangely confident, without knowing why,
that he would not be saying a word to Lynette about
his non-Paris weekend, and how disastrous his 'fun'
weekend had turned out to be. As for telling Lynette
herself, still not finished with cringing yet, Ashlie
knew that whatever lies she had to tell about her
weekend away, that never would *anybody* hear the true
facts of it from her lips.

Feeling like going home and going to bed and
staying there for however long it took for the ache in
her heart to heal, she left work that night, not looking
forward to when Lynette arrived home, and the fake
surprise she would have to show when Lynette told
her she had not, after all, been to Paris.

When Ashlie reached the flat though, she was to see
from Lynette's parked car that she was not going to
have to wait for her to arrive home. Clearly, Lynette
had not been able to face going to work that day.

But her surprise that contrary to her surmise
Lynette had not gone to her office, was not the only
one that awaited Ashlie. She had fully expected her
sister-in-law to be looking as fed up as she herself was
feeling, but when she had just inserted her key in the
door lock, the door was pulled back. And as she raised
her startled eyes, she was to see a sparkly-eyed
Lynette standing there, with such an aura of supreme
happiness radiating from her, that it was to put her in
mind of Lynette on her wedding day.

'What . . .' Ashlie broke off, unable to believe her

eyes, a delight starting to break within her as Lynette moved to one side. A tall mousy haired man stepped from behind the door and into her line of vision.

'And why weren't you here to greet me on Friday, kid?' he said severely. A moment later Ashlie was launching herself at him, and his severe expression had collapsed and given way to a huge grin.

'What are you doing here!' she squeaked, when her adored brother had let go his bear hug.

'It's a long story,' he replied, his eyes going from her to rest on his wife with a look of love.

'When did you arrive? Why didn't you let us know you were coming? How long can you stay?'

Questions had poured from her then, Ashlie reflected as she lay in her bed that night. And 'Whoa!' Norris had grinned. But over a meal most of her questions had been answered. And although she had never got to hear of the ins and outs of the 'long story' she had knowledge of two very definite facts. That Lynette and Norris were still as much in love as they had ever been. And the other—that Chase Marriner was nothing more than a double-dyed rat!

Ashlie had learned that, with Norris unaware of his wife's infatuation with another man, he had arrived in England on Friday morning, where his first action, before he left the airport, had been to ring Lynette. Whereupon an overjoyed Lynette, on hearing that he was home for a few days only and that he would be flying back to Brazil on Wednesday night, had promptly arranged some time off to be with him during his short stay, and had arrived at the flat only a little after him.

Which, Ashlie thought, was really terrific from their point of view. But since Lynette could not have been at the airport to meet Chase on Friday, it meant that for all his 'I should risk telling her while there was still time for you to practise a little double dealing?' that it was not he who had told Lynette that the Paris weekend was cancelled, but Lynette, by not turning up, who had called the weekend off. Which left it more of a certainty, than a doubt, in Ashlie's mind, that Chase had never, from the start, intended to follow through his 'I'll take you if you like'. For had Lynette been at the airport on Friday night, then without question, Ashlie saw then, it would have been Lynette whom Chase would have gone away with.

Double dealing! My stars, she fumed, had she been played for a fool! Why, had it not been for Norris coming home so unexpectedly last Friday, then Chase, with Lynette sat beside him, would have been smirking his arrogant head off all the way to Paris, while she, muggins Ashlie Holman—had Mrs Parry not tipped her off that he had gone to the airport— would have sat waiting like a spare dinner in the drawing room of Clarendon House.

She doubly cringed about the way she had been with Chase last night. Unfolded before her lay the facts that with Chase never having any intention of telling Lynette 'It's all over' he had found Lynette's sister-in-law a most convenient second string. With his weekend in Paris well and truly gone for a burton, he'd had no trouble finding himself a playmate for the weekend, had he? All he'd had to do, the fickle rat, was to return to Clarendon House where he knew that he still had his 'fun' weekend in the bag—his second string—just sitting there waiting for him.

Serve him right that the weekend had turned out so disastrously. She was glad, glad, glad, that it had been such a fiasco. Though her brow puckered at the memory of how, when she had put up no 'resistance' it had been he who had called a halt to their lovemaking. But, cringing again, Ashlie was to hurry over that episode, and a few seconds later she was back to calling him a low, contemptible, lying swine.

That she too had told some fair old whoppers, was, she justified, all in a good cause. For with Norris thinking she had been with her parents at the weekend, when he had got around to asking, 'How are the folks?' she'd had to rapidly go into the fields of invention herself. Though it was more lies by implication, when she had replied,

'They're fine. We weren't in Whittledene at the weekend. We went to the Dales. Mum and Dad are still there actually. You know how they love the Dales.'

'Um,' he said, swallowing wholesale, since he had no reason not to, that it had been her parents she had gone away with. 'That explains why I couldn't get a reply to any of my phone calls.'

That Norris would be back in Brazil by the time her parents returned from their holiday, and would not have been in touch with them, gave Ashlie small relief. But when finally sleep claimed her, she was still no nearer to finding an answer to how she was going to keep Lynette from having a phoned conversation with them. With her mother so taken with Chase, she would no doubt tell Lynette what a lovely surprise it had been to bump into her employer when Chase had been taking Ashlie to meet his mother.

The next few days dragged by with interminable slowness. For no matter what names Ashlie found to call Chase Marriner; her love for him was still there. Even though she would tell herself countless times that the way he had taken her for a ride should have killed every emotion in her, but hate, stone dead, it had not. Being truly in love, she was painfully discovering, was totally different from being merely infatuated.

But if the days for her were going at tortoise pace, then sensitive to Lynette and Norris, she was aware that for them their short time together was speeding by on wings. Aware that they needed no one else, she had made herself scarce during Norris's brief stay. But she was in the flat on Wednesday night to say goodbye to him before Lynette drove him to the airport.

'Have a good flight,' she said as she hugged him.

'You take care,' he advised solemnly. Then with an attempt at humour which in the circumstance of his pending parting with Lynette she knew he was not really feeling, 'There are big bad wolves out there just waiting to gobble up pretty girls like you.'

'Yes, Grandfather,' she replied. But she didn't know for whom she was crying after he and Lynette had left—Norris, because he had gone and she might not see him again for ages—or herself, because she had met one of the biggest of wolves, and it just wouldn't stop hurting.

Lynette, she saw from her reddened eyes when she came back from the airport, had been crying too. 'Come and sit down,' she said gently, pushing aside her hurt in the face of Lynette still being distressed, 'and I'll go and make you a drink.'

Wordlessly Lynette shook her head. 'I think I'll go to bed,' she mumbled, and, with tears coming to her eyes, she fled.

Lynette had got her sorrow out of her system the next morning. Or, at least by the time she joined Ashlie for breakfast she was more in control and able to speak without the fear she might burst into tears half way through a sentence. But, just as Chase had been Ashlie's waking thought, it was clear that Norris was uppermost in Lynette's mind and, that she wanted to talk about him.

'The time will soon go by,' said Ashlie, knowing that it wouldn't, but trying to help.

'I don't think I can stick it out until Norris finishes his contract,' Lynette answered. Ashlie was instantly fearful but Lynette, catching her alarmed look, found a smile and told her, 'Don't look so worried. Norris and I aren't heading for the divorce courts. It's just that, while I'm not in any way domesticated—and Norris knows that I'd crawl up the wall at any suggestion that I spend the rest of my days playing "the little woman stopping at home"—he's suggested that if I spend my June holiday in Brazil he'll try and get some leave too, then while I'm there I could look around the nearest city to where he's working, with a view to finding out what short-term career prospects are available to me out there.'

'You'd give up your job with Marriner's!' Ashlie exclaimed in astonishment, aware of how much Lynette valued her job.

'Well, not without a great deal of thought,' she answered. Ashlie felt as if she was on a see-saw of wondering how much thoughts of Chase Marriner would have to do with her sister-in-law's decision.

'Lynette,' she said, the words trembling there on her tongue and just having to be voiced, 'about this— thing you have with Ch-Chase Marriner . . .'

'Lord, is that the time!' Hurriedly Lynette reached for her briefcase. But she had heard Ashlie's question, and she was still friendly as on her way out, she promised, 'Unless my desk is piled high, I should be home fairly early tonight—we'll have a nice long talk about it then.'

Ashlie was to wish she was half as career-minded as

her sister-in-law that day. For at the end of her secretarial day, she had to admit that she had found her work exceedingly dull. Though she was to acknowledge as she let herself into the apartment, that she had never felt her work to be particularly dull before, that perhaps it was only since she had brushed shoulders with never-a-dull-moment Chase Marriner, that not only her work, but everything she had done since, had seemed positively flat.

As she had promised, Lynette was home fairly early. But she seemed in thoughtful mood. Their meal was spent in desultory conversation, all subjects touched on but the one Ashlie was most interested in. Lynette kept drifting off for long minutes now and again, and not saying anything.

Believing Lynette's thoughts to be centred on Norris, and that, hating to be apart from him, she was having a terrible inner struggle when it came to throwing up her job to be near him, Ashlie decided that this was not the moment to remind her how she had said they would have a talk about Chase.

Though she was to find out that she had not forgotten. For, appreciative of how exacting was Lynette's work, and how tired it sometimes made her, when Ashlie said, 'Why don't you go and put your feet up in the other room, and I'll bring the coffee in,' Lynette gave her an affectionate smile.

'I'm a selfish bitch. I don't deserve a super sister like you.'

'I only offered to make the coffee!' she exclaimed, but Lynette's warmth had pleased her.

A few minutes later she carried the coffee into the sitting room, she found that Lynette was ready for a chat. Norris was obviously to the forefront of Lynette's mind for it was of Norris whom she spoke first and Ashlie was glad. Though she was to be little short of amazed when, opening, her sister-in-law began to tell her something of the 'long story' that had been instrumental in bringing Norris home for those few short days.

'His first thought when he needed to get in touch with me, was to get to the nearest place where he might find a phone,' Lynette began. 'Then Norris got to thinking that since any call he made could quite well be one of those crackly ones which would have him tearing his hair out in frustration, he decided that he might as well go the whole hog, and take a few days' leave.'

While not wishing Lynette to tell her anything that was private between her and Norris, Ashlie could not help from wondering why Norris had needed to get in touch with Lynette other than by letter. Then she recalled how she had once had occasion to wonder with Lynette never seeming to be home, how she ever found time to write to him. Hesitantly she questioned Lynette.

'Did he need to make contact with you because—you'd stopped writing?'

Lynette shook her head. 'It wasn't that I'd stopped writing,' she explained, 'but more . . .' she was the one to hesitate. But then as open as ever, she went on, 'But more that the tone of my letters had changed.'

'Chase Marriner?' Lynette looked as though she would make an instant denial, and for a moment Ashlie thought she was going to be less open than she had hoped.

Though she had obviously changed her mind about denying that she had ever had a fling with him, even so, Lynette's honesty ducked the question by replying to the query.

'It wasn't only my letters that were off key, but your letters to Norris also.'

'My letters!' Ashlie exclaimed. 'But,' she protested, 'I never said a word about you and Ch . . .'

'I know,' said Lynette. 'But when Norris looked for reassurance in your letters that all was well, all he found was more cause to disturb him. Where once what you wrote seemed to consist almost entirely of what you and I were doing together, the places we visited and where we'd eaten   you know better than I what you wrote—there was a sudden lack of such information in your last few letters. That combined with my correspondence to him being—well, more than a little miffy, I suppose,' she owned, 'built up to have him unable to ignore the feeling that something was very definitely wrong.'

'And that's why he came home so unexpectedly?'

Lynette nodded, and then sighed, 'Oh Ashlie, I'm missing him already, and he's only been gone twenty-four hours.'

Ashlie smiled her sympathy, her heart gladdened to see such evidence of Lynette's love for her brother. But, since hardly a word had they spoken of the serpent in the undergrowth, she still needed to hear from Lynette's own lips that she would not again forget where her true love lay.

'This—attachment—you formed for Chase Marriner,' she said. 'It *is* over, Lynette, isn't it?'

Solemnly Lynette looked at her. And Ashlie thought she was going to explain how it had been. Certainly she expected more than the, 'I was an idiot, wasn't I,' which she eventually, did say. That was the total of their 'nice long talk about it'. Lynette then moved away from the subject of Chase, her eyes starting to sparkle in enthusiasm, as she began again.

'Apropos the possibility of my getting fixed up with a job I can get my teeth into in Brazil, yours truly has today booked up to take a crash course in Brazilian. Or rather the language of the Brazilian,' she laughed. 'From now until June, Monday and Thursday evenings will see me hard at it trying to assimilate Portuguese!'

Chase Marriner's name did not come up between the two of them in the following few days. But if his name was never on Ashlie's tongue, then it was seldom that Chase was out of her mind.

When no telephone call came from her parents at the weekend to say that they were back, she guessed that, taking advantage of a vast improvement in the weather, that they were extending their holiday to include an extra weekend. It was a relief to have another few days in which to think up what she was going to say to them.

She was toying with the idea as she drove home on Monday of saying how she had fallen out with Chase and, that since he was Lynette's ultimate boss would they not mention they had been going to see his mother, or mention that they had seen them together at all, so that Lynette should not feel awkward in any dealings with him. But when Ashlie reached the flat, all thought was taken out of her head when she was greeted by the sight of the most magnificent bouquet of flowers she had ever seen.

For witless moments, she just stood and stared at the spendid floral tribute that lay, where it had been delivered, outside the flat door.

Then, dropping her bag and her bits of lunch time shopping down, she stooped to find the card that had come with it.

'Chase,' she read. Just that one name, and no more.

No message, or anything else, just 'Chase,' but it was enough to make her heart go wild.

For all of ten wonderful ecstatic seconds, Ashlie floated in a delicious dream world in the unthinking belief that Chase had sent this marvellous floral tribute to her. To send her above the realms of ecstasy, she saw through her overjoyed tear-filled eyes, that there was even the most beautiful perfect red rose at the centre of the arrangement.

Her joy was not to last. For thundering in to send her crashing down from the top of a Mount Everest of ecstasy, came the memory that she was not the only female who lived at her address.

But, unable to come to terms with her crushing disappointment, even as common sense tried to tell her that Chase would not send her flowers, all the same she had to look to see to whom they were addressed. She turned the card over—the reverse side was blank.

But the flower-edged florist's card, was enough to tell her that if on that previous occasion he had sent some minion to the florist's with his signed card and his order, this time, the signature the same—so keen was he—he had gone to the florist's personally.

Jealousy, pure and simple took possession of her then. And before she knew what she was doing. Ashlie had torn the card in half. But, unrepentant, her jealous thoughts going furiously one after the other, she saw that there would not need to be a name and address on the card, would there? Lynette's address was already known to the delivery man, and it would be impossible to get this tremendous delivery mixed up with the rest of his calls. It would be only once in a blue moon that they had a delivery as splendid as this one.

She came down from being ecstatic with delight one

moment, to knowing bitter, earth-shattering, disappointment the next. That, being closely followed by unrestrained jealousy; the next emotion that was to assault her, was one of total outraged fury.

As plain as day was the fact that Lynette must have told Chase she was more interested in keeping faith with her husband than she was in having an affair with him. The flowers, she fumed, Chase not being able to accept no for an answer, were nothing more than an attempt on his part to weaken Lynette's resistance.

Her fury was increased when Ashlie recalled how easily he had weakened her own resistance. In the next moment she was charging down to the dustbin. And sacrilege though it was, she broke the stems and, her anger giving her strength, she rammed the flowers in to the bin, and slammed the lid down hard. Perhaps when Lynette did not thank him, it might give him the idea that when her sister-in-law said no, she meant no.

Her first flurry of fury had gone when Ashlie let herself into the apartment. And it was then that she was able to see that as she had yelled at Chase that it had never been her intention to sleep with him when they had gone away, he had decided that any 'I owe you that much' agreement he'd made to leave Lynette alone, could be declared null and void.

Lynette, when she came in, was in a tearing hurry to get to her Portuguese class. But she did find time to pause and to stand and swallow down the sandwich and coffee Ashlie had ready. She sweetly, suddenly proved she was not the selfish bitch she had claimed when, not having a moment to breathe, she noticed that Ashlie was a little on the quiet side.

'Is there something the matter?'

'Lynette,' said Ashlie, no time to choose her words since Lynette didn't want to be a second late for her first lesson. 'If—if Chase Marriner—came after you again—you wouldn't . . .'

'Oh, Ashlie, love,' said Lynette gently. And strangely then—she just wasn't an openly demonstrative person—to Ashlie's surprise her sister-in-law came over and gave her a quick hug, and even kissed her cheek. 'Forget that—other business,' she said then. And taking up her briefcase now loaded with a quantity of brand new text books she added, 'There's only one man for me.' Smiling she went towards the door, 'And I'm married to him.'

Lynette had hardly gone out of the door when the phone rang. And Ashlie, still with nothing convincing enough prepared, felt her spirits sink to rock bottom to hear her mother's voice.

'I bet you thought we'd emigrated,' she started off brightly, and went to chatter on to explain, as Ashlie had rightly assumed, how they had taken advantage of the turn to spring weather, even though spring wasn't officially here yet, to extend their holiday by an extra weekend. The part Ashlie had been dreading all too soon was upon her when hopping back to exclaim about how appalling the weather had been the first few days of the holiday, her mother told her, 'I was terribly worried that you and Chase might come to grief, what with the roads being so dreadful and everything. But your father said he was sure you would be all right, and that Chase looked to be capable of handling any situation which might arise.'

'He is,' said Ashlie, only just holding down a sour 'standing on his head' as she thought of how quickly able he had been to switch from one female to another.

'Did you have a good visit with Mrs Marriner?' Joan Holman queried, her polite way of asking 'What's his mother like?'

'Actually,' said Ashlie, her palms beginning to sweat, 'we didn't see her. We hadn't gone far when Ch-Chase saw that, with the bad weather setting in, there was a blizzard raging when we left the hotel,' she inserted, 'we might get stranded and not be able to get back for Monday. So he booked us into a couple of rooms at the next hotel we came to, and we started out for London early on Sunday morning.'

'Oh what a shame!' exclaimed her mother, and her feelings going out to Chase's mother, 'Mrs Marriner would be so disappointed not to see her son—you too of course,' she hastily tacked on.

'Talking of sons,' said Ashlie quickly, rapidly pushing to the back of her mind the memory of Chase, all aggression, saying, 'I've never taken any woman home to "meet mother" yet'. 'Guess who was here when I got back?'

Ashlie was to wonder when she put down the phone why she hadn't mentioned Norris's visit from the outset. For with her mother dreadfully disappointed to have missed him, and firing one question after another at her about him, it had taken her mind completely off what had been her prime topic of interest at the start.

Ashlie was still trying to eject Chase and his wretched bouquet from her mind while taking the cover off her typewriter the next morning, when Gillian Rogers popped into her office to ask how she felt about going to see Julie Grant straight from work.

'I'd love to,' said Ashlie, and grateful to have something else to pin her thoughts on for a while, 'Julie's out of hospital now, isn't she?'

'Came out at the weekend, and convalescing at home,' agreed Gillian, going on to tell her where Julie lived, and how to get there.

'It seems daft with you living so close to me for us to take two cars. Why not leave your car in the car park,' Ashlie suggested, 'I can drop you off at your place when we've seen Julie, and pick you up in the morning.'

'Great idea,' said Gillian, and, as her boss walked past the open door, 'I'd better go before "sir" starts hollering for me.'

That Tuesday turned out to be one of those days when one needed to do ten things at once. Ashlie was glad to be busy, but as busy as she was it did not stop thoughts of Chase from slipping in. She was in her car with Gillian and driving along before she remembered that she had not, as she had intended, telephoned Lynette to advise her that she would be home later than usual.

Julie was pleased to see them, her sense of humour having come through her operation with her, all three of them collapsed in laughter when during their visit she went into a vivid description of how modesty had been stripped from her when strange men—men she had never seen before mark you, and dressed in white coats one and all—came to her bed and insisted on taking the most diabolical liberties with her person.

Ironically Ashlie was herself cheered by the convalescent they had gone to cheer. And when on the way to drop Gillian off, Gillian suggested she might like to stop off and have a bite to eat and a cup of coffee, Ashlie agreed in the vain hope that perhaps if she got out more, it might be instrumental in easing the torment of spirit which loving Chase had brought.

They were driving in the area where she lived with Lynette when Ashlie thought to make a small detour.

'I'll just pop in and tell Lynette where I am,' she explained, though she guessed that Lynette would be knuckling down to her Portuguese homework by now.

But Lynette was not studying her language course. She was standing at the outside entrance to the block of flats. She was not alone.

CHAPTER NINE

At first, Ashlie saw neither the man nor the woman as she turned into the street where she lived. But to spot Chase Marriner's parked car was enough for every vestige of good cheer to rapidly depart.

Scarcely able to believe her eyes; needing to make doubly sure that the sleek dark vehicle was his, Ashlie slowed down. Then it was, that she saw Lynette—and Chase!

But Lynette had spotted her too. And from the way Chase quickly spun about, she must have said as much to him. Ashlie did not wait to see what happened next. For, feeling as though she had just been kicked in the stomach, in the next moment, she slammed her foot down hard on the accelerator.

'Hey!' exclaimed Gillian, to remind her she had a passenger.

'Sorry,' she apologised, vaguely aware that she had been instrumental in making Gillian's head jerk back. 'I—thought we were going to hit a cat.'

'Thank goodness you missed it,' said Gillian.

And it was only a few minutes later that Ashlie was having to call the non-existent stray cat into use again, when Gillian broke off something else she was saying, to exclaim, 'You've forgotten to stop at your flat!'

'So I have!' exclaimed Ashlie. 'That perishing cat must have taken it from my mind. Not to worry, Lynette will probably think I've gone to the cinema straight from the office.'

Another two hours went by before Ashlie thought

she would be overstaying her welcome if she remained at Gillian's flat for much longer. Though, for all she felt an aversion to going home, she would not be persuaded to stay longer when Gillian said, 'It's still early yet.'

Having re-affirmed she would pick Gillian up in the morning, Ashlie drove slowly back to where she lived, knowing without a shadow of doubt that if Chase Marriner's car was still where she had seen it, that she would spend a night in a hotel rather than go in.

Lynette had looked dressed to go out for the evening, she recalled, without effort, as she dawdled along. Which had to mean she had arranged beforehand for Chase to call and pick her up.

There was no dark sleek car there when Ashlie reached the flat. Fury mingled with heartsickness as she got out from her Mini. How *could* he be such a swine? How could Lynette be so two-faced that, regardless of her avowed love for Norris, she could actually let Chase come to call for her!

Not expecting to find Lynette at home, Ashlie let herself in, and was shaken to see her sister-in-law sitting at the table, with her pile of text books open in front of her, looking as though she had been hard at it all evening.

But, having had the wool pulled over her eyes once too often, Ashlie was in no mood to easily believe what Lynette wanted her to believe.

She was not sure if she was capable of speaking to Lynette in any way civilly. Lynette though, on seeing her still angry expression, left what she was doing and, as if not quite knowing how to start, said simply, 'Trust me. Just—trust me.'

Giving her credit that she was not going to pretend she had not seen her when she had been leaving the flat with Chase, Ashlie's tone was short none the less.

'You've been out with him.'

'No. No, I haven't,' Lynette denied.

'You've had him up here! In this flat you've shared with Norris!' Appalled, jealousy was chipping in with its share of bitterness.

'No!' Lynette denied sharply. But, her tone softening, 'Chase merely called on—a business matter. He didn't come further than the front door.'

It could well be, Ashlie thought, that she was again being a gullible fool, but she was persuaded by the sincere look of Lynette, backed up by the reams of hand-written notes on the table by her open text books, that she was telling the truth. Chase, had not put one foot inside the flat.

Though when she argued that he'd had all day in which to discuss business without the need to call, Lynette repeated, 'Ashlie—trust me.' And the affection that had grown in her for Lynette had her swayed to believe that while it was blatantly obvious that Chase was after her, Lynette had really meant it when she had said, 'There's only one man for me, and I'm married to him.'

She was to have further proof the next evening though that Chase, whatever rebuffs he was getting from Lynette, was not giving up. Ashlie had barely got in from work, and had not yet put down her shopping, when the phone rang. She nearly collapsed when, his voice even, controlled, she heard Chase.

'How are you, Ashlie?'

All kinds of emotions were in that moment to run riot within her. She fought hard to find some of that same control she could hear in him, but knew it was a losing battle. She wanted Chase to love her, and only her, and her control had little chance when jealousy attacked, and went on the rampage. Anger joined in.

'Anything you have to say to *Mrs* Holman,' she spat furiously down the phone, 'can be said during business hours. My sister-in-law is just not interested in receiving calls from you at home.'

'Did I say I was ringing to speak to Lynette?' he asked, his tone short, abrupt.

Almost then Ashlie would have weakened. She knew she would have been overwhelmed with joy had it indeed been her he had telephoned to speak with. But, the abrasive way in which he had asked his question, was to give her the stiffening she needed. And there was no let up in her fury then.

'You've got a nerve! Any time Lynette isn't available you think you'll keep your hand in by sharpening your technique on me. Well I've got news for you Mr-self-appointed-God's-gift-to-women-Marriner,' she said hotly. She was aware that he was trying to get a word in but she was not allowing him that much—he'd made a fool of her before. 'As I may have told you, I've been inoculated against the likes of you,' she stormed on. 'So if mine is another name you've got jotted on your—your *availability list* for future reference, then let me tell you, that I have no wish now, tomorrow or *ever*, to speak to you again, to see you again, or to ever have any contact with you at any future date.'

The next moment she had slammed down the phone. A second after that, she was in her bedroom howling her eyes out.

Wondering if the day would ever dawn when she would return to being the girl she had been before she had met Chase Marriner and had every one of her emotions thrown out of gear, Ashlie got out of bed the next morning and gritted her teeth. She was not, she decided firmly, going to spend the rest of her life languishing for a man who just did not deserve that anyone should waste a second pining for him. For all of a minute and a half, her resolve worked.

It was while she was doing the lunch-time shopping that, having brought pork chops for dinner that night, Ashlie realised that with Chase sitting there right on her shoulder, she had forgotten that today was Thursday. Lynette, keen to get to her Portuguese lesson, was not going to have time that evening for more than a hastily grabbed sandwich

Though when Lynette did come home, she was later than she had been on Monday, and did not have time for even a sandwich. And in so much of a hurry was she, she only had time for a cursory ''Lo Ashlie,' as she raced by to dive into her bedroom to empty her briefcase and to refill it with her text books.

Less than a minute later, a loud wail of anguish, made Ashlie charge in through Lynette's open bedroom door. Her heart pounded in fear that the least that had happened was that Lynette had tripped over in her hurry and had broken a leg.

'What's wrong?' she asked, her fears subsiding when she saw Lynette standing on both her legs and apart from wearing a look of despair, appearing to be physically all right.

'This,' cried Lynette, distractedly taking a large buff-coloured envelope out of her briefcase and waving it in the air. 'I should have given it to the messenger for special delivery.'

'Is it important?' she asked, and saw from Lynette's abstracted look that it was. She was torn in two, Ashlie could tell.

'Oh, hell, it's vital that it's handed over tonight,' she groaned. Swearing expressively, Lynette then came to what was obviously a reluctant decision. 'There's nothing for it,' she said, hurling the offending envelope angrily back into her briefcase, 'I shall have to take it personally.'

'Will you miss much of your class?' Ashlie asked, no end cheered to hear how much importance Lynette placed on her Portuguese lessons, and sorely wanting to offer to deliver the envelope for her. But she guessed that it would contain highly confidential matter, and thought not to embarrass Lynette into having to explain that while she trusted her, it was more than her career was worth to let anyone who hadn't been screened by Marriner Security Systems to so much as get their finger prints on the envelope.

Absently Lynette nodded, 'I'll probably miss the whole of my lesson,' she grieved. 'Wouldn't you know something like this would happen just when I need to cram in all the tuition I can, if I'm to get anyone to take me on when I get to Brazil.'

Warmed through and through by what she had said, Ashlie almost rushed in to risk any embarrassment that might ensue, by offering to deliver the package in her stead. For, by the sound of it, when faced with the choice of furthering her career in England, and the chance of finding work in Brazil where she could be nearer to Norris, it seemed that Lynette had definitely made that decision which she had said would need to be given a great deal of thought.

'I can't afford to lose so much as half an hour of my lessons,' Lynette went on unhappily. 'Not if I'm to get the hang of the language before I go. Just when . . .'

'Let me take the envelope for you.' Ashlie could hold back no longer. 'That is,' she added less impulsively, 'if you think it would be all right for me to take it.'

Lynette had looked startled by her interruption. But there followed no embarrassed explanation of why she could not take her up on her offer. A sudden beaming smile coming to Lynette's mouth.

'Would you?' And when Ashlie nodded eagerly, 'You're a darling,' she accepted gratefully.

Speedily then, already delayed and not wanting to miss more of her class than she could help, she tossed the envelope out of her briefcase and on to her bed, and frantically stowed away her textbooks. And Ashlie was to have further evidence of how much to do well in her lessons meant to her, in that when Lynette had raced out of the door, she had to rush after her to remind her that she hadn't got a clue to which address she was to play postman.

'Where do I take it?' she called with a laugh.

Lynette was going helter-skelter down the stairs when she called back, 'The address is on it.'

The smile lingered on Ashlie's face when she went back inside the apartment and closed the door. And she still felt a glow of warmth that while Lynette had always been supremely efficient, her love for Norris could make her so hare-brained.

Donning her car coat, she had her car keys in her hand when she went into Lynette's bedroom to collect the envelope from the bed. She anticipated that her journey would most likely be to the home of Lynette's immediate boss, Mr Fowler. But all sign of a smile was to go from Ashlie, and every scrap of warm feeling was to go with it, when, on turning the envelope over, she saw, to whom it was addressed!

Ashlie was frozen rigid where she stood, unable to move or to even think. It was not Mr Fowler's name before her disbelieving eyes, but right there beneath the red 'Strictly Confidential' tab, in Lynette's own writing, were the words, 'To be handed personally to Mr Chase Marriner only'!

Colour drained from her face. Ashlie had no need to read the address—she already knew it. She had been there before!

If her first reaction on seeing to whom she had to deliver the envelope, had been one of horror, then Ashlie's second reaction when it came, was to be one of refusing point blank to go anywhere near Clarendon House that night. For all of fifteen minutes then, she thought up a dozen very good reasons for the package still being in the flat when Lynette returned from her class.

But, realising how vitally important the contents of the envelope must be if her sister-in-law had been prepared to miss one of those lessons that meant so much to her, made Ashlie leave her flat on reluctant feet and go towards her car.

Even so, with Clarendon House coming nearer and nearer with every mile it was touch and go whether she would arrive there or not. Had she not been constantly prodded by visions of Lynette looking absolutely flabbergasted—not to say livid—that she had been wrong to entrust her with such a pressing errand, she would have turned her car around and have gone back the way she had come.

As it was when she turned into the drive of Clarendon House, regardless that the instructions were quite clear and that the buff envelope was to be handed to Chase personally and none other, Ashlie was hoping with all her heart that Mrs Parry would be the one to answer the door.

Relying on it not taking more than a few seconds to get rid of her urgent cargo, Ashlie left her car keys in the ignition, and walked over gravelled ground that had been snow covered the last time she had seen it.

Then, wanting to be away from her surroundings as fast as she could, she climbed the steps and rang the bell.

She had only moments to wait before she heard sounds from within. Either Mrs Parry had been in the vicinity of the front door, or Chase, impatiently watching the clock for the important documents to arrive, had been listening for the bell to ring.

It proved to be Chase who pulled back the door, a pent-up expression apparent on his face until he saw that the envelope had arrived. As his face went expressionless, she reminded herself to keep her own face from showing any emotion.

'Lynette said that this had to be in your keeping tonight,' she said coldly, and thrust the package at him, her feet already executing an about turn.

But, the package in his hold, her intention to go down the steps never got past but a movement in that direction. Butterflies took off in her stomach as she felt the firm grip of his hand on her wrist.

'Surely you'll come in for some refreshment after your drive,' said Chase evenly, that grip on her wrist bringing her round to face him.

Her heart joining in the general free-for-all of turmoil within, weakness invaded as her eyes took in a trace of strain on him that told of how dreadfully hard he must work. But, as coldly as she was able, she refused his suggestion.

'Thank you, but no . . .'

Weakness was to go flying, alarm there in its place when, still a man who was unprepared to take no for an answer, Chase suddenly growled, 'Stop being so bloody stubborn, and come in.'

He was not waiting for her to refuse again. She was quite unprepared for the tug he gave to her wrist and, shaken, Ashlie found she was standing in the hall with him.

Before she could get her breath to ask him what the hell he thought he was playing at, he had uncaringly tossed down the highly confidential documents she had brought to a hall table. 'You've never been afraid to cross my threshold before,' he muttered as he ushered her along the hall and into the drawing room. Only then, did he let go his hold on her wrist.

Ashlie was bombarded by memories aroused by seeing the flames licking at the logs in the hearth. There had been a log fire the last night she had been here. She and Chase had lain before it. They had kissed and ... She snatched her thoughts back, and was then desperately trying to get herself together. Chase, obviously from his 'You've never been afraid to cross my threshold before' somehow knew of her feelings for him. Ashlie felt fear tremble within her.

'Take a seat,' he invited, 'and tell me what you'd like to drink.'

Coldly Ashlie looked back at him. 'I'll take neither a seat nor anything to drink,' she replied. And just in case he thought differently, 'I want nothing from you,' she troubled to inform him.

From the way his jaw clenched, she guessed that there was something sarcastic on its way. But his reply inspired immediate alarm.

'I'm fully aware of that. Just as I'm fully aware of what it is you *do* want. A pity the man you love isn't the settling down type, isn't it?'

Panic made great swiping darts at her. Quickly she lowered her eyes to the carpet. That Chase had indeed seen that she loved him, had her ready to bolt. But the instinctive desire she felt to take flight, was quashed when she realised that it was not himself Chase was referring to—though he, too, was not 'the settling down type'—but Kevan Salter.

'And we both know what you want, don't we?' she said, raising her eyes ready to serve him her parting shot before she got out of there. 'What you want is anybody's wife, not one of your own. A pity,' she bounced back at him, 'that Lynette is very much in love with her husband, isn't it?' And, for good measure, as she made her way towards the door. 'You'd better chalk Lynette up as the one who got away, Chase. Since Norris came home . . .'

'I'm not remotely interested in your sister-in-law,' sliced through what she was saying, and hit her as she reached the door. 'I never have been.' The denial made Ashlie spin round, angry at this fresh evidence of what a lying swine he was. 'Not before, or after her husband returned for those few days, did I ever look on Lynette Holman in the way you suggest.'

'My God!' Ashlie exclaimed—he was even managing to *look* sincere! Not so much as a blink could she see as he faced her. 'That,' she stayed to say, 'just has to be the most blatant lie I have ever heard.'

'I'm not lying,' he retorted. 'I . . .'

'Not much you're not,' she said heatedly, wondering why it should hurt so much that he could tell her a barefaced lie. She had every evidence of what a smooth talker he was. 'Apart from your pursuit of Lynette all this week, you seem to have forgotten that I know—since I was the one you proposed to leave high and dry—all about your intended little Paris venture with her.'

'There was no Paris venture,' Chase cut in sharply. He then threw her an exasperated look. Her astonishment peaked. Even when he *knew* that she knew the facts were indisputable, he was still intent on lying. 'Well, there was a Paris trip planned,' he owned, as in Ashlie's book he had to, 'but . . .'

'Keep your buts,' she said tartly, wondering what it was about him that had her still loving him. 'I'm just not interested in your lies.' Hastily she turned her back on him. But her hand had done no more than to reach for the door handle when roaring about her ears came Chase's bellow.

'*I'm not lying!*'

Ashlie might, while her ears were still ringing, have quickly exited then. Only in a few rapid strides, Chase was over at the door with her, his hand coming to her arm, his voice quieter though still showing a large degree of irritation. 'Oh, for God's sake come and sit down and *listen*,' he said tersely.

'Why should I?' she asked aggressively, but just the fact of his nearness, of his hand on her arm, had her resistance wilting.

And, when it seemed her feet had no intention of going anywhere but out through that front door, her agitation mounted when Chase did not appear to be likely to move from her or let go of her until she had done as he said. Her weakness for him had her allowing him to lead her to a settee near to the fire.

But when Chase stepped back, and seemed to need a few moments to invent fresh lies, Ashlie found she still had enough aggression left, to charge on waspishly.

'Well—why should I listen to anything more you have to say?'

For a moment longer Chase silently looked at her. Then, quietly, he said, 'Because—I've deceived you over a number of things, I've . . .'

'You can say that again,' she butted in, and saw from the way his brow came down that her interruption was not favourably received. He otherwise ignored her interruption though.

'I want you to listen to me, Ashlie, because I've been made to realise that—I'm just not going to get anywhere with you unless I can work from an honest basis.'

Get anywhere with her! Staggered, disbelieving, the only translation which Ashlie could immediately make of what he had just said, was that, bluntly, Chase had just announced that he wanted an affair—*with her*! That, or, her thoughts were quickly racing then, was it that Chase—with his desire for an honest basis—was still after Lynette? Could it be that Lynette, the break with him never made at all, had thought up a way to get her to Clarendon House purely so that the ever inventive Chase could feed her some plausible tale, which she was to be gullible enough to swallow, to excuse him and Lynette going away together for weekends ad infinitum!

Her racing thoughts began to slow down when she recalled how convinced she had been that Lynette loved Norris and had no room in her life for any other man. Thoroughly confused then, Ashlie saw that there was only one way to find out what Chase was up to.

'I see,' she said at last. Then, went on, 'Perhaps, for starters—and since by the look of it you're intent on voyaging in the new seas of honesty—maybe you'll be honest enough to tell me if the envelope which Lynette had me believing would have the whole Marriner empire crumbling if it wasn't delivered tonight, was as urgent as I was led to believe it was.'

He had not liked her sarcasm, she could tell from the glint that had come to his eyes. Though, sensing that an attempt was about to be made to make a fool of her for the umpteenth time, Ashlie was past caring what he liked or did not like as she waited for his *honest* answer.

CHAPTER TEN

DETERMINED she was just not going to have the wool pulled over her eyes again, Ashlie waited long moments as Chase studied her rebellious face. She could see him silently deliberate about the best way to go about doing just that.

'The package you brought,' he then began, 'was urgent.' Ashlie, remembering how carelessly he had tossed it to one side, thought she might just as well go home now if this was the sort of honesty she was to be served. 'Not from a business point of view.' Warily she eyed him as she waited for the rest of it. 'More important,' he continued, 'was the fact that it was you who should deliver it.'

'So it was a set up!' Not giving herself time to wonder why he should so openly admit she had been hoodwinked into tearing over to Clarendon House, hotly, Ashlie charged on. 'You, with Lynette's connivance, thought to get me here so that—forgetting I'm immune to your charm—you could have a stab at lulling my fears about the affair the two of you are . . .'

An explosive, 'For God's sake, listen to me and not your vivid imagination,' cut her off. 'Didn't you hear me when I told you that I'm just *not interested* in having your sister-in-law as my mistress.' He was still denying an interest in Lynette, but he caught at control, and his voice was quieter when, speaking every word clearly, he said, 'I am not now, nor have I ever, had an affair with Lynette Holman. Nor,' he added succinctly, 'have I ever so much as contemplated having an affair with her.'

That he sounded so sincere, set misguided joy leaping in Ashlie. But promptly, she came to her senses. Wasn't that the sole reason that this elaborate ruse had been used—to hoodwink her?

'You'll be telling me next,' she retorted disagreeably, 'that you don't even like her.'

'I don't have to like her,' he returned sharply. 'She works for me. But while I admire her work and her dedication to her career, that's as far as it goes.'

Angrily Ashlie again stamped down the impulse to want to believe him. 'Which is why,' she flared, 'you rewarded her "dedication to her career" by deciding to take her on a *non-business* trip to Paris.' She saw he was ready with an answer to that too, but she wasn't having any. 'And don't tell me again that there was no Paris venture,' she rushed on hotly, 'because Lynette was toting a case when she left the flat that Friday morning. I was there—I *saw* it!' she ended aggressively.

'I don't give a damn what you saw,' Chase barked. Though he did concede, and Ashlie couldn't see how he could avoid doing so, 'Had your brother not arrived home unexpectedly, then Lynette would have gone to Paris. But,' he said before she could get her word in, 'definitely, not with me.'

If she had been angry before he added that rider, her temper was certainly to soar sky high at that statement. As a cover for their affair, he was trying to make her believe that Lynette had taken up with some entirely new man.

'How dare you try to fob off the affair you want with her on to some other man?' she flew then. 'I saw her all sparkly eyed about you, before she told me about you and her . . .'

'I don't care how sparkly eyed she came across,'

Chase stampeded in shortly. 'Take it from me that whatever you saw, was only what Lynette wanted you to see. That whatever she told you about her and me had no truth in it, but was only what she wanted you to believe.'

Stunned that he could say such things and sound so utterly convincing, Ashlie could not but wonder what she was doing still sitting there.

'Now why would Lynette want to make me believe she was on the way to having an affair with you, if she wasn't?' she scorned. She didn't wait for his reply, though she didn't doubt that he had an answer. 'Isn't it far more likely that, as I'm her sister-in-law, I'd be the last person who she would want to know what was going on? As it was, it was only because she couldn't conceal what was going on when night after night she came home late . . .'

'It's precisely because you *are* her sister-in-law, that this whole mess started,' he sliced her off.

Ashlie tried to make sense of that, but found herself confused. 'You're too devious for me,' she said sourly, 'I've lost you somewhere.'

More confusion came her way when Chase, leaving some space between them, sat down beside her on the settee. It was then she knew, from the changed rhythm of her heart when he looked at her and held her eyes, that no matter how devious he was being, she stood no chance of falling out of love with him.

'I was lost, too, to know what Lynette was about,' he said quietly then. 'Which is why, when she returned to her office last Thursday, I interviewed her and demanded to know down to the last detail, what the hell she was playing at.'

'Lynette told you, of course,' she prompted, wading deep in confusion, as she invited more lies.

'After a reluctant start.' As expected, Chase obligingly took up her invitation. 'But she could see she would be without her job and her beloved career—in my organisation anyway—if what she told me was less than the truth.'

'You threatened to sack her?' she asked, still searching around in the mists to find out where all this was leading.

He nodded. 'Then it was I got out of her that she is deeply in love with the man she married.' He paused when Ashlie shot him a startled look, then went on, 'Having met, married, and said goodbye all in a matter of months, she had been having the most unhappy thoughts that her husband did not love her.'

'But Norris thinks the world of her!' Ashlie exclaimed, that fact alone clear as she forgot completely how certain she was that Chase was hell bent on laying a false trail.

'She knows that now she has seen him again,' said Chase. 'But apparently, what with the hours she put in when the change over of offices was underway, together with her single-minded determination to justify her promotion—she placed herself under pressure, and had little left for rational thinking in her personal life.'

'Poor Lynette,' murmured Ashlie, seeing only then the agony of mind her sister-in-law must have gone through.

'That wasn't what I called her,' he muttered. Then resumed, 'Her first thought when doubts about her husband's love began to creep in, was to fly out to Brazil to find out where she stood. But as her doubts began to take a firmer hold, she came round to the view that with her promotion so recent she couldn't take time off, and, that should things be the way she suspected, more than ever then would she need her career to hang on to.'

Having come so far away from not being prepared to believe a word he said, tears stung Ashlie's eyes, at the dreadful torment Lynette had been through; when flashing in came her own memory of that time when, according to Chase, Lynette had been ripped apart by doubt.

My God! And she'd nearly fallen for it! There was no sign of tears in Ashlie then, as she wasted not a moment in letting him know that he had fooled her for the last time.

'That Norris might have fallen out of love with her didn't seem to bother Lynette when she went to a party with you and didn't come home until two the next morning,' she shot at him acidly. 'Nor did she show much sign of missing her husband when after the party, your flowers arrived.'

'I can explain all that,' said Chase, his tone gone gritty as he realised that any softening there had been in Ashlie had not lasted very long. 'Just accept for the moment that Lynette Holman can be a supreme actress when she's after something.'

Not prepared to accept anything, not without proof anyway, she was suddenly to see all the proof she needed of Lynette's supreme acting ability. She had easily taken her in when she'd acted out coming across that 'vitally important' *forgotten* envelope, hadn't she?

'Might one ask,' she said sceptically, still wary and not ready to trust him an inch, 'what it was exactly my sister-in-law was after, in trying to make me believe she was well on the way to having an affair with you?'

Her tone not lost on him, it surprised her that he was going on with it. But he was, though his reply when it came was to replace her scepticism with pure astonishment.

'Just this,' he said. 'Having decided she could not go to Brazil, Lynette, desperate for some assurance of her husband's love, began searching for some way which, if he thought anything of her at all, would have him rushing home to her. The way she found,' he said after a brief pause, 'was through you.'

'Through me!'

'It was you who gave her the idea she needed when—after several of us had gone for a meal after a late working session—you asked had it been just the two of us. From that, the notion came that if she fed you a load of guff about me being the new man in her life, that you, loving your brother, as I too know you do, would waste no time in writing to tip him off. In the light of which, if love her he did—he would come home.'

Absolutely astounded, Ashlie just stared. 'But—I didn't breathe a word to Norris,' she said faintly.

'Instead,' said Chase softly, a small smile breaking, 'you came to me. And I,' he said, that smile vanishing, 'while basically objecting most strongly to some female I'd never heard of daring to come to my home to harass me over something of which I was not guilty, was torn,' he paused, then continued, 'not to fight some devil that urged you should be played along for your impertinence.'

Warm colour flushed to her face as her thoughts winged back to that first meeting, when, if he was to be believed, it was the first he had heard that he was having an affair with Lynette! She had called him a callous swine, Ashlie remembered, and he had called her an insolent bitch. Oh God, she thought, part of her wanting to die from embarrassment, while part of her wanted to rejoice that the man she had given her heart to, was not the monster she had thought him.

She was near to begging his forgiveness then that for one moment she had thought he had any intention of taking Lynette away to Paris. Suddenly though, as if someone had just poured a bucket of cold water over her, Ashlie came to her senses.

Abruptly, not intending to listen to another word, she stood up from the settee. 'Ingenious,' she said frigidly, ice-cold anger in charge. 'But not ingenious enough.' And with that, her heart feeling fractured and in tiny pieces, she marched to the door.

But only to find that Chase had got there before her. 'What the hell do you mean—ingenious?' he demanded, anger about him, too, as he barred her way.

They stood toe to toe and glared at each other. Ashlie was of a mind not to answer. But when it became obvious that short of crowning him, and that was a tempting thought, he was not going to move, she coldly told him, 'You nearly had me believing *your* guff.' Though the ice in her had started to crack, she went gamely on. 'Shame your housekeeper knew you were at the airport on the night I arrived with my weekend case, wasn't it?' A hurt fury broke from her. 'Had Lynette been at the airport you'd have flown off with her and laughed all the way that green little Ashlie Holman was sitting in your home waiting for you.'

'I knew before I got there that Lynette wouldn't be at the airport,' Chase tried to tell her.

'My God—you're slipping!' Ashlie retorted, angrily hitting his hand away as he tried to take hold of her arm. 'Everything else you've so far said has been just this side of credible. But don't insult my intelligence by trying to get me to believe—all set as you were for a cosy weekend for two in Paris—that you knew in advance that the woman you intended to go with, wouldn't be there to take off with . . .'

'I wasn't taking off,' Chase chopped her off sharply.

'Huh,' she scoffed, not sure she wouldn't be crowning him yet if he didn't soon move from the door.

'For your information,' he said, throwing her a savage look, 'the only reason I went to that damned airport, was to bid *adieu* to a loyal team who'd worked all hours God sent to get a top security move smoothly accomplished.'

'I'm not int . . .' Ashlie stopped midstream, the part of her that still wanted to believe him, catching at her. 'You weren't going to fly?'

'I've asked you to listen to me, Ashlie,' said Chase, his aggression gone at her quieter tone. 'It's—important to me,' he added gently, 'that you hear me out.'

She had no idea why it should be important to him that she heard him out. But his gentle tone seduced her to unprotestingly be led back to the settee, her only protest made when sitting with him closer to her this time.

'Don't—tell me any more lies.'

'Every word I've told you this evening, has been true,' he promised. She did not argue, but sat waiting solemnly for him to go on. 'I suspected it was going to be difficult—that I was not in for an easy time,' he said. 'But I've said I can explain, and since I can see that you're not convinced of my veracity by anything I've so far said—I'd better go back to the start.'

His nearness was affecting her again, and Ashlie tried for a return of her former spirit, but her, 'I'd be pleased if you would,' had little of the sarcasm to it which she had tried for.

'As you already know,' he began without further prompting, 'about a half dozen or so employees worked extra long hours while the change of premises project was under way. I took an interest in what was going on myself, though other work having a greater priority, it was only occasionally that I showed my face.'

'Only occasionally?' Ashlie questioned.

'I'm pretty tied up most of the time,' he informed her, 'so it was only occasionally that I could go to give what support I could. Occasionally too, when I'd missed dinner, I'd join them for something to eat. Never,' he added, 'were there less than three or four of us taking time out to eat.'

'You're saying that—you and Lynette—never dined when it was—just the two of you?'

His look unswerving, 'That's what I'm saying,' he replied levelly.

About to argue the point, she saw that if Chase was not leading her up the garden path now, then she had certainly been led up it before. But, in the hope of being able to decipher exactly what lay at the top of that garden trail, Ashlie swallowed down any desire to argue. And Chase observing she had changed her mind about saying something, went on.

'I was with the team on the night of the project finally being completed. It was late,' he told her, 'but that didn't stop us from adjourning to the nearest hotel to celebrate. The next day I had flowers sent to the two women executives involved in the show, and to the wives of the male executives.'

Ashlie opened her mouth to exclaim that Lynette had said she had been to a party with him the night before his flowers with their 'Thanks for everything' message had arrived. But with Chase again making it all sound more than credible, all she said was, 'I'm—listening,' not certain that, while wanting to believe him, she wasn't leaving herself wide open.

'However,' he continued, 'it seemed to me that raising our glasses in a late-night session in a hotel, and sending flowers to the ladies, wasn't much of a thank-you for all that had been achieved. I instructed a bonus to be paid, of course, but it was when I considered the hours that had been put in, hours when husbands and wives hadn't seen much of each other, that I offered them a weekend away somewhere on the company.'

'They—er—chose Paris?' The question had slipped out though she had not meant to say an enquiring word until he had finished.

Chase nodded. 'They're a close-knit bunch, but even so I would have thought they'd have had enough of each other. They surprised me by opting to have a collective weekend in Paris. I,' he added, 'went to the airport to see them off. All,' he amended, 'bar one.'

'Lynette?'

'My secretary had phoned through to enquire if there were any last-minute panics they needed help with. The message I got back was that there were no problems, but that Mrs Holman's husband had unexpectedly arrived from Brazil and that she preferred his company to theirs, and that she had already started her weekend, and was extending it until Thursday.'

Her insides suddenly all of a quake, many memories were there to press her to believe all that Chase had told her. There were Lynette's 'miffy' letters to Norris, her own 'off key' letters to him, all instrumental in bringing him home—as Lynette had wanted. And surely Lynette must love Norris, or why else would she be swotting like mad to learn Portuguese?

She became aware that while Chase waited for her to make up her mind what to believe, he was showing that same sign of strain which she had noticed earlier. But what Ashlie could not fathom, was why, unless he had a conscience about the way both he and Lynette had taken her for a ride, it should matter to him whether she believed him or whether she didn't? Which brought her back to her suspicion that he and Lynette must have plotted some elaborate cover to fool her.

'Why?' she asked then, bringing out about the only thing in the whole plausible tale that didn't fit. 'Why, if all you've said is true, couldn't Lynette have told me herself? Norris went back over a week ago. And,' she went rushing on when Chase would have interrupted, 'if, as you say, you—carpeted—her for making me believe she was going away with you when she wasn't, then since you've obviously told her how I'd—I'd—been to see you, then she's known since last Thursday that she could come clean and explain everything to me without any need to play act about that envelope or to get me to come haring over here.'

Breathless when she came to a full stop, Ashlie stared at Chase in amazement as he replied, 'Lynette told you nothing, because I told her to say nothing. I—was still working a few things through. I needed time . . .'

'I'll bet you needed time to work a few things through,' she flared, amazement gone as the significance of his last remark hit her. 'Like, for instance, how to cover why Lynette was still "working late", when according to you, the work she was doing had ended on that night she came in at two in the morning.'

'If she stayed out late after that, then it must only have been to give credence to the affair she was supposed to be having,' he replied. 'God knows where she went,' he said aggressively, 'but it certainly wasn't anywhere with me.'

'Of course it wasn't,' Ashlie blazed. Fury with him shook her when, flashing before her eyes, came the vision of him standing with Lynette outside the flat—only this Tuesday. She rose swiftly to storm from the settee and out of his house.

She did not make it past getting to her feet before he had caught hold of her and pulled her back to sit beside him. 'Now what bee have you got under your bonnet,' he rapped, holding her down as her hands tried to lash out at him.

'Damn you!' she shrieked. 'Let me go!'

'Like hell I will,' he snarled. 'You're here tonight because I've exhausted all other ways of getting through to you. You're here so I can clear up this whole bloody mess. And now you're here,' he roared, 'you're not going *anywhere*, until the last doubt in your mind is answered. From there,' he gritted, still grimly holding on to her, 'we'll have . . .'

'We!' she yelled. She had no certain idea what any of this was about, but a definite feeling inside that somehow in his scheme, whatever that might be, Ashlie Holman was lined up to play piggy in the middle. 'We nothing,' she went on, 'I'm not going to listen to anything else you have to say. I'm not, I'm not,' she said, shaking her head. 'I've heard all I'm going to hear from you. I prefer instead to heed the evidence I've seen. Evidence there in the flowers you sent Lynette only this Monday, not to mention the red rose at the centre. Evid . . .'

The bellow that came from Chase, about the only

way he could make himself heard above her yelling, had Ashlie hushed and staring. 'What—did you say?'

'I said,' he replied, still holding on to her, though she was no longer struggling to be free, 'that the flowers I sent last Monday, were not for Lynette—they were for you.'

'For me!' Though stunned to hear him say that the fabulous bouquet she had so furiously squashed into the dustbin had been for her, Ashlie was soon back to challenge. 'Then why wasn't my name on them?'

'How the hell do I know?' he exploded. 'It was your name I gave them.'

But Ashlie could not believe him. 'How ill-mannered of me not to ring you on Monday evening to thank you,' she snapped sarcastically.

'I knew by five-past-nine on Tuesday morning that you'd dumped them in the dustbin.'

From that, she gathered that Lynette had disposed of something on her way out on Tuesday, and had been able to tell him there was no room in the dustbin, when he'd rung through to ask her if she had liked the flowers.

'You came round to the flat that night to ask me why I'd done it, I suppose?' she queried.

Her sarcasm was not going down very well, she could see. But, 'It *was* you I came round to see,' he agreed. 'Lynette had told me you'd be in, and that . . .'

'So you *are* in this together,' Ashlie accused, wrenching her hands out of his grasp.

Chase threw her an exasperated look. But that he was still trying to get her to believe him only underlined for her, when she knew how impatient he could be, that he must be hell bent on pursuing the woman he was after.

'Only in so far,' he curtly agreed, 'that in return for

her co-operation,' Ashlie's brow going up did not deter him, 'I promised, should she still be career minded when she and her husband return from Brazil, that I'll find her a position in my organisation on a par with the one she has now.'

'You—know—she's thinking of working in Brazil?' she blinked. 'Lynette's told you that she misses Norris so much that she may leave England to be near him?'

'I guessed it was likely when I got out of her what she had been up to,' he told her. 'All I needed on Tuesday to have her co-operation, was to dangle the carrot of her re-instatement.'

'Co-operation?' Her head was starting to spin. But if she hoped that any answer Chase made would clear it, then she was left staring, and more muddled than ever when, his eyes steady on her face, he continued.

'I needed to see you, Ashlie.'

'You—needed . . .'

'I'd sent you flowers only to learn they had not been well received. It was then I told your sister-in-law to forget what she was doing and come straight to my office. It didn't take long for me to have her agreement that, in return for my promise about her job, she would leave me alone with you when I called that night to see *you*.'

'You—wanted to—tell me, all you have tonight— personally?' she asked, wishing her dull brain would wake up and tell her why he should want personally to tell her when Lynette could just as easily have done so.

'I needed everything cleared away about how you've been deceived before . . .' he broke off, but light, disappointing light was beginning to dawn, when he went on. 'When I saw your car pick up speed when you saw me outside your flat with Lynette, I knew that not only would you not be returning while my car was anywhere about; but also that I was going to have the devil's own work in getting to you at all to do any clearing up of past deceptions.'

Comprehending at last, a woodenness had taken charge of Ashlie when, confirmation not needed, she asked, 'It was me you wanted to speak with when you rang last night, wasn't it?'

'I was trying to tell you that, but the whole time you were giving me an earful,' said Chase. 'Devil's own work was a misnomer for the hard job I saw I had in front of me when, after telling me you neither wanted to hear from me, or see me, you crashed the phone down in my ear.'

She had known in advance the type of man he was. She knew she had no call to feel wounded—but she did. Ashlie nevertheless managed to rise above the hurt she was feeling. It was coldly then, that she stated, 'So this morning, you again enlisted Lynette's aid. This morning, determined that I would see you, you dreamed up that urgent-envelope farce.'

'Short of kidnapping you,' he replied, his eyes narrowing at her cold tone, 'I couldn't see how else I was going to get you to hear me out. I have discovered, Ashlie,' he said, his tone suddenly softening as his hands stretched out to take a hold of hers, 'that I don't want us—to end.'

For a few wildly crazy moments, even though by then she knew exactly what he was meaning, her heart forgot to listen to the intelligence her head was trying to impart. And for ageless seconds, as her green eyes stared into his, all manner of emotions were let loose inside of her. But those moments were brief, and her head soon took charge again.

'I—see,' she said slowly, understanding what she had to do. The way she felt about him, she knew that if she did not get out now, her strength would not hold up to deny what he was asking. 'Thank you, Chase, for telling me all you have,' she said, her voice a shade rocky. 'I—appreciate that—contrary to my doubts, you are, after all—a man of your word—and ... and that my fears, about you and Lynette are groundless and that—they have always been groundless.' She had to pause to take a long breath when she felt her small control begin to slip. 'But, with regard to—my having an affair with you—I'm ... I'm just not ...'

'An affair!' Chase cut in, sounding taken aback.

But Ashlie, while admitting that when it came to being fooled, she had been a sitting target, was not of a mind to be fooled ever again. And, ignoring his show of amazement, she turned to face him, her voice icy.

'I may have a lot to learn, Chase, but if I haven't just been propositioned, then I can't think what else you intended to imply by your statement that you "don't want us to end".'

'Oh, God,' he groaned, 'I've said it all wrong.' And when she was drawing on all the dignity she could find to get up and quietly leave, 'Listen to me, Ashlie,' he said.

But she was shaking her head. 'I've listened all I'm going to listen,' she told him, her voice icy still. She tried to get up to go, but found that his grip on her hands had tightened.

He was still refusing to let her go when she heard him mutter, 'Oh, to hell with it.' Then, quickly, he was saying, 'Once that other mess was out of the way, I'd meant to lead up slowly to find out how—things—are with you.' Fiercely she tugged to be free, but his hands were still gripping her. 'Since you must believe that I've made one hell of a fool out of you, I'll just have to take it if you laugh your head off when I make a fool of myself, and tell you . . .' he halted, the words to make a fool of himself getting stuck.

But that somehow Chase thought he might make a fool of himself, when she had only ever known him on top in everything he did, surprised Ashlie into forgetting for the moment her urgent desire to be away. She was still wary enough of him to collect herself though and hid her surprise. She braced herself not to bend a millimetre, lest he was using some other ploy to get her to agree to a meaningless affair.

'I confess, a laugh on you would be something of a change.'

'I had that remark coming, and more,' he agreed. 'Though, believe me, I never thought to do more than string you along for a short while at the start.' And, giving her no chance when she looked likely to interrupt, 'I was wrong, totally wrong to take you away as I did,' he owned. 'But, in truth, I didn't expect to see your car parked outside and you sitting here with your case waiting for me, when I returned from the airport that night.'

'Oh, come on!' she exploded, not pleased that he thought he could tell her any lie he chose and get away with it. 'You were . . .'

'On my honour,' Chase cut in, 'I felt certain you'd have got from Lynette by then that there was no "affair", and that I wouldn't see you come Friday—I was doubly certain I wouldn't be seeing you when I knew that your brother had arrived.'

'Because—you thought, with Lynette ecstatic to see him, that—I'd know that not only was her weekend with you off, but, consequently, that there was no need for me to go away with you either?'

'Exactly,' he said. 'But as soon as I recognised your

car outside, I knew my thinking had been wrong. Not only had you not been home from your office where you would have seen your brother, but also, unless you'd had a phone call from him, you didn't know that he was home at all.'

Shaken, Ashlie felt her face flood with colour that, not expected by Chase, she had been in his home, with her weekend case, when he had arrived. But then she remembered the way he had acted when he had come home. He'd shown not a glimmer of surprise. She once again felt anger boil up to overwhelm and quell her embarrassment. Hotly, she laid into him.

'Rake is too good a name for you,' she spat, enflamed with rage. 'You couldn't resist it could you? You just couldn't resist that here was some female who'd called to offer herself on a plate for you. You couldn't . . .'

'It was precisely because you *were not* offering yourself on a plate,' he cut in, 'that when I might have owned up, I found that I—didn't want to.'

'You fancied the challenge?' she snapped, not liking to remember how little of a challenge she had presented when once he had kissed her.

'Call it a quirk in my nature,' Chase replied, 'but you were such a new experience for me. I found that the same sharp-tongued female had returned, pretending she was going to honour an agreement, which I knew damn well she had no intention of honouring—if she could help it.' Ashlie could have done without his last comment. 'I was caught, intrigued to discover just how you intended to have me honour my side of the bargain, while at the same time—you dishonoured yours.'

'You—louse,' she hissed.

'I deserve that too,' he accepted, without heat. 'But,

In my defence, it never once occurred to me that you might be a virgin, and must have been going through all kinds of mental agony on that drive up north. Just,' he added, a warm note there, 'as it never occurred to me that I should be so charmed by you when we stopped for lunch, that for the rest of that drive I was stabbed by doubt about the wisdom of what I was doing.'

Vividly, Ashlie remembered that lunch. *She* had been charmed by *him*. They had laughed together, and afterwards in the ladies room, she had known she was in danger of falling in love. They had both been silent for the rest of that drive, she recalled. But that the reason for his silence had been because he was starting to have doubts, was, to put it mildly, something of a surprise.

Having heard him state he had been charmed by her, had weakened her, forcing her to fake an aggression which was no longer there.

'There wasn't much sign that you'd been "charmed" when you bellowed that a cup of tea had more appeal than me,' she said belligerently.

'I was as angry as hell that you'd flinched back from me,' said Chase, not rising to her show of aggression. 'I was angry with myself, too, that it should disturb me. I was still angry when I came back,' he admitted. He paused, tension suddenly there in him. Looking at her, looking into her eyes, and nowhere else, quietly, quite out of the blue, he said, 'But when I went into the bedroom and looked down at your beautiful sleeping face, all anger left me. And I knew then at that moment, what it was that had excited me, that had stimulated me, and what it was that had seen me going against what I knew to be the right thing to do that Friday—I,' he said softly, 'had fallen in love with you.'

Staring at him in utter, stunned astonishment, had Ashlie been able to murmur a sound, she had no idea as her brain seized up and her heart began clamouring, what she would have said. For long witless moments she just stared into his never more serious face, what he had just said, echoing and re-echoing, in her head. She was still staring at him, thunderstruck, when, his expression tense still, Chase spoke.

'Can I hope, Ashlie, since you aren't breaking up at this chance I've given you to have the last laugh, that you don't, as I deserve, totally hate me?'

Still stunned, sorely needing confirmation that she had not misheard him, when Ashlie did find her voice, strangled though it came out, it was not with an answer to his question but a question of her own.

'Y-you—love—*me*?'

'I do,' he replied without hesitation. 'Even as afterwards I fought against it, I knew it then. And what I now know is that, while I want and desire you with a need such as I have never known, I want and need you in other ways. That I want to keep you, to protect you, to cherish you . . .'

'To—love me?' she asked, not surprised at the breathless sound to her voice.

'Above all, to love you,' Chase agreed softly. 'I want to drive from you all thought and feeling for the man who opened my emotions to include jealousy when I heard him call you "darling". I want . . .'

'Kevan Salter?' she choked. 'You were jealous of Kevan?'

'Are you still in love with him?' he abruptly countered, jealousy there for her to see in the sharp way he said it.

'I—I don't think I ever was.'

'Thank God for that,' he said fervently. But, having

quickly disposed of Kevan Salter, Chase was gripping her hands. 'Is there a chance for me with you, Ashlie?' he asked then. 'Is there a chance, now you know that villain though I was to take you away, I'm not the marriage-wrecking villain you thought me. Can you,' he asked, his grip on her hands intensifying, 'find it in your heart to—love me a little?'

With not a thought in her head to where all this was leading, all Ashlie wanted to do, having heard him say that he loved her, was to tell Chase that she was so deeply in love with him that even when she had thought him a double-dyed villain, she had not been able to change that. But shyness, sudden, and unexpected, was to cleave her tongue to the roof of her mouth, and all she could do, was to nod.

'You—do—love me a little?' he asked, her nod not sufficient for him.

'M-more—than a little,' she found her voice to tell him. 'I—love you with the whole of my heart.'

In a moment Chase had let go his hold of her hands to haul her into his arms. Still not convinced he asked urgently, 'Is it true?' And pulling back so he should see into her eyes, 'Tell me it's true,' he urged.

'It's true,' Ashlie complied gently, wanting him to believe it. 'There were signs before, but I knew definitely that I was in love with you on the night you checked us out of the hotel my parents were staying in.'

'Oh God,' Chase groaned, holding her fast against his heart, 'have you been through the same desolate agony of mind that's woken with me every morning?'

'And taken to bed every night,' Ashlie concurred.

Minutes ticked by then. As though starved, they clung to each other and kissed. And kissed again. She could feel his heart beat matching the heady pulse of

her own. And there was no let up on that feeling when
Chase, with one hand warm at the side of her throat
and the other at her back, breathed.

'Oh, my love, this is where you belong. This is
where I wanted you last weekend. I ached for you, and
wondered what the hell you were doing over in your
flat when I wanted you here with me. It was then,' he
confessed, 'that I finally admitted what I'd been hell
bent on not acknowledging all that week.'

'Might I ask, what that was,' she asked, her heart
bumping that Chase had felt that same ache for her,
that she had felt for him.

'It was then I knew,' he said, his lips taking time out
to whisper lingeringly across hers, 'that the sharp-
tongued female who'd walked into my life and shown
that, while I could get a reaction from her when I held
her in my arms she just didn't want to know
otherwise, was the woman I had to have.'

'Is—that why you sent that beautiful bouquet on
Monday? So I should ring you and . . .'

'You had me not knowing whether I was on my
head or heels. I was afraid if I came after you and told
you of my all-consuming need for you, that I'd soon
be on the receiving end of something I didn't want to
hear. It was then I decided I was going to have to be
patient, and try my inexpert hand at a little old-
fashioned courtship.'

'But—I dumped your flowers in the dustbin.'

Chase smiled. 'It was because I didn't want you
upset by thinking you'd made a fool of yourself, that I
told Lynette to keep quiet about how your efforts to
save your brother's marriage had been totally
unnecessary. But by Tuesday, I knew that if I was
going to get you to marry me, that the truth would
have to come from me. When you crashed the phone

down on me on Wednesday, I knew that if I couldn't think of a way round it, I was never going to see you again, much less get your consent to be my wife.'

'Er . . .' said Ashlie, as he came to an end, her heart racing fit to burst, 'you've—just asked me to—marry you.'

'That's right,' said Chase. And with his look gently adoring, he continued, 'Didn't you understand, my darling, when I said that this is where you belong, that I meant, you belong here as my wife?'

'But—but . . .' she tried, then managed to string a few more words together. 'But you enjoy being a bachelor. You—you said . . .'

'I know what I said, and it was true, I did enjoy the freedom of being a bachelor,' he agreed. 'I was still telling myself during the first few days after you'd left my home without so much as a breakfast cup of coffee, that I wanted to go on in the same way I'd always gone on.'

'But you—discovered differently?'

His smile said 'And how.' As if never again did he want her to misunderstand him, freely, he then admitted, 'It was my view when I cut short our weekend away, that once I was back in more familiar surroundings—and away from you—that I would soon come to my senses. But,' he gently kissed her cheek, 'a week away from you, is a year in my heart's calendar, dear love. In that year-long week I was to discover that what I thought was a fear of becoming entangled—and which had me booking us out of one hotel and into separate rooms in another—was not fear, but a feeling of being so bowled over that I didn't know where the hell I was at.'

'And you know—where you're at—now?'

'You've given me too many sleepless nights—the

first being that night in my separate bed—for me not to know that I can't take life without you, my heart.'

Their lips met in a kiss. And unable to deny their need of each other, minutes were to tick by, the only sound in the room the crackling of logs in the hearth, as they sought to assuage the ache they had both known.'

And there was a fire burning in Ashlie too, a fire reflected in Chase's eyes, when he at last pulled back, a gently teasing curve coming to his mouth.

'You're surely not going to have the nerve to turn down my proposal after *that*, are you?'

Ashlie grinned, but she was unashamed of her heated response. But Chase had given her a few seconds in which to get together a tenderly teasing question of her own.

'Do I get to "meet Mother"?' she asked.

A delighted laugh broke from him. 'Like— tomorrow,' he said.

Her laughter joined in with his. 'We could maybe tell her of our engagement,' she murmured.

Joy lit his eyes to hear she had just accepted his proposal. 'Oh, my darling,' he breathed. 'We'll do better than that, my dearest love,' he said tenderly, 'we'll take her an invitation to our wedding.' And with his joy overflowing, in the next moment, he had Ashlie held close up against his heart.

Coming Next Month in Harlequin Presents!

839 BITTER ENCORE—Helen Bianchin
Nothing can erase the memory of their shared passion. But can an estranged couple reunite when his star status still leaves no room for her in his life—except in his bed?

840 FANTASY—Emma Darcy
On a secluded beach near Sydney, a model, disillusioned by her fiancé, finds love in the arms of a stranger. Or is it all a dream—this man, this fantasy?

841 RENT-A-BRIDE LTD—Emma Goldrick
Fearful of being forced to marry her aunt's stepson, an heiress confides in a fellow passenger on her flight from Denver—never thinking he'd pass himself off as her new husband!

842 WHO'S BEEN SLEEPING IN MY BED?—Charlotte Lamb
The good-looking playwright trying to win her affection at the family villa in France asks too many questions about her father's affairs. She's sure he's using her.

843 STOLEN SUMMER—Anne Mather
She's five years older, a friend of the family's. And he's engaged! How can she take seriously a young man's amorous advances? Then again, how can she not?

844 LIGHTNING STORM—Anne McAllister
A young widow returns to California and re-encounters the man who rejected her years before—a man after a good time with no commitments. Does lightning really strike twice?

845 IMPASSE—Margaret Pargeter
Unable to live as his mistress, a woman left the man she loves. Now he desires her more than ever—enough, at least, to ruin her engagement to another man!

846 FRANGIPANI—Anne Weale
Her sister's offer to find her a millionaire before they dock in Fiji is distressing. She isn't interested. But the captain of the ship finds that hard to believe....

Readers rave about
Harlequin American Romance!

" ...the best series of modern romances
I have read...great, exciting, stupendous,
wonderful."
                    —S.E.*, Coweta, Oklahoma

" ...they are absolutely fantastic...going to be
a smash hit and hard to keep on the
bookshelves."
                    —P.D., Easton, Pennsylvania

"The American line is great. I've enjoyed
every one I've read so far."
                    —W.M.K., Lansing, Illinois

" ...the best stories I have read in a long
time."
                    —R.H., Northport, New York

*Names available on request.

You're invited to accept 4 books and a surprise gift Free!

Acceptance Card

Mail to: Harlequin Reader Service®

In the U.S.
2504 West Southern Ave.
Tempe, AZ 85282

In Canada
P.O. Box 2800, Postal Station A
5170 Yonge Street
Willowdale, Ontario M2N 6J3

YES! Please send me 4 free Harlequin American Romance® novels and my free surprise gift. Then send me 4 brand new novels as they come off the presses. Bill me at the low price of $2.25 each —an 11% saving off the retail price. There are no shipping, handling or other hidden costs. There is no minimum number of books I must purchase. I can always return a shipment and cancel at any time. Even if I never buy another book from Harlequin, the 4 free novels and the surprise gift are mine to keep forever.

154 BPA-BPGE

Name	(PLEASE PRINT)	
Address		Apt. No.
City	State/Prov.	Zip/Postal Code

ACAR-SUB-1

Readers all over the country say Harlequin is the best!

"You're #1."

A.H.*, Hattiesburg, Missouri

"Harlequin is the best in romantic reading."

K.G., Philadelphia, Pennsylvania

"I find Harlequins are the only stories on the market that give me a satisfying romance, with sufficient depth without being maudlin."

C.S., Bangor, Maine

"Keep them coming! They are still the best books."

R.W., Jersey City, New Jersey

*Names available on request.